HOT LEAD.
BURNING VENGEANCE.

"What's the verdict, Doc?" Fargo asked.

"Your wound wasn't caused by hitting your head when you fell."

"What caused it, Doc?"

"A bullet," Adams said. "Somebody blew you right out of the saddle, Fargo."

"I remember, " Fargo said.

And suddenly he did. It came back to him. He had heard the shot and reacted a split second too late. A man of lesser reflexes would not have reacted at all and would have been killed. Fargo threw himself from his saddle at the sound of the shot, causing the bullet to crease his skull rather than imbedding itself in it.

"Whoever did it," Doc Adams said, "must have thought you were dead. They didn't bother to check."

"That was their first mistake," Fargo said. "Their last was stealing my horse. They're going to pay for both."

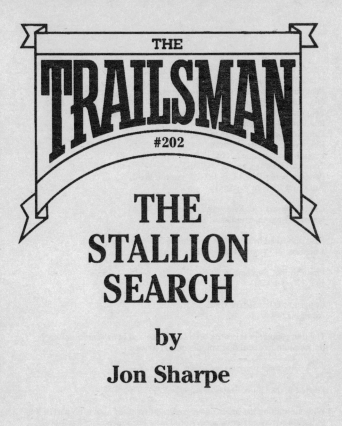

THE TRAILSMAN

#202

THE STALLION SEARCH

by

Jon Sharpe

A SIGNET BOOK

SIGNET
Published by the Penguin Group
Penguin Putnam Inc., 375 Hudson Street,
New York, New York 10014, U.S.A.
Penguin Books Ltd, 27 Wrights Lane,
London W8 5TZ, England
Penguin Books Australia Ltd,
Ringwood, Victoria, Australia
Penguin Books Canada Ltd, 10 Alcorn Avenue,
Toronto, Ontario, Canada M4V 3B2
Penguin Books (N.Z.) Ltd, 182-190 Wairau Road,
Auckland 10, New Zealand

Penguin Books Ltd, Registered Offices:
Harmondsworth, Middlesex, England

First published by Signet, an imprint of Dutton NAL,
a member of Penguin Putnam Inc.

First Printing, September, 1998
10 9 8 7 6 5 4 3 2 1

The first chapter of this book originally appeared in *Salmon River Rage*,
the two hundred and first volume in this series.

 REGISTERED TRADEMARK—MARCA REGISTRADA

Printed in the United States of America

The Trailsman

Beginnings . . . they bend the tree and they mark the man. Skye Fargo was born when he was eighteen. Terror was his midwife, vengeance his first cry. Killing spawned Skye Fargo, ruthless, cold-blooded murder. Out of the acrid smoke of gunpowder still hanging in the air, he rose, cried out a promise never forgotten.

The Trailsman they began to call him all across the West: searcher, scout, hunter, the man who could see where others only looked, his skills for hire but not his soul, the man who lived each day to the fullest, yet trailed each tomorrow. Skye Fargo, the Trailsman, and the seeker who could take the wildness of a land and the wanting of a woman and make them his own.

*1861, the newly formed Nevada Territory,
where some men feel it is their right
to take what they want,
even another man's horse . . .*

1

Skye Fargo couldn't move his legs.

This greatly concerned the big man, who assessed his situation and was surprised to find that he was lying on hard-packed ground. He had no idea how he had come to be here, or even where "here" was. He knew his name—which was, at least, of some comfort—but not much more than that.

One thing quickly became clear. Along with not being able to move his legs, his head was pounding. He put his hand up to touch it and it came away sticky and red. All right, at least now he knew where the initial wound was, but that didn't explain why he couldn't move his legs. Maybe he just wasn't trying hard enough. After all, he was able to move his arms, and his hands—he flexed his fingers and found that he could move all of them, as well.

He took stock of himself and noticed that he was still wearing his gunbelt, and his Colt was still in the holster. Whatever had happened to him happened so fast he hadn't been able to react. This was also of some concern, but he could deal with that later.

He reclined on his back and stared at the sky. The sun was going down, so it was going on evening. What was the last thing he remembered? A hot sun, right overhead, so that meant he'd been lying here for some hours. Also, he'd been riding his horse. He lifted his head and looked around, but he could not see the Ovaro. It was not like the animal to wander off.

He returned his attentions once again to his legs. Pushing himself up onto his elbows, and then to a seated position, he used his hands to feel his legs. They did not feel particularly damaged. In fact, there was no pain in his legs at all—there was nothing. A cold, hard ball formed in the pit of his stomach as he realized he could not feel anything in his legs at all. He could see that he was squeezing them with his hands, but his legs could not feel the fingers that were handling them.

Panic was not something Skye Fargo was conversant with so it did not even occur to him that this was what he was feeling. However, he did know that he was greatly concerned. He still wished he knew where he was, and why he had come here . . . wait. That was it. He remembered something. He was in the Nevada Territory, which had only recently been formed and named. He tested his memory. Recent discoveries of silver and gold along the eastern slopes of the Sierra Mountains in Western Utah Territory had made it necessary to form a government that was in keeping with the needs of the twenty thousand people who had flocked there to make their fortune. Hence, the creation of a new territory from pieces of an old one.

But why was he here?

And what the hell was wrong with his legs.

He suddenly felt very fatigued, as if the act of sitting up had tired him out. He gently lowered himself onto

his back again, and stared at the sky above until an un-
natural darkness flowed over him. . . .

He felt as if the ground beneath him was moving,
undulating. Also, the sound of voices came to him. He
frowned, listening. It sounded like a man and a
woman, but he couldn't understand what they were
saying. Concentrate, he told himself, concentrate.

". . . like he might be waking up."

"See if you can get him to talk, find out who he is?"
a man's voice asked. The first voice had been a
woman's, but deep, throaty.

He opened his eyes and found himself looking into
a beautiful face etched, at the moment, with concern.

"Can you hear me?" she asked. "Can you understand me?"

He licked his lips and said, "Yes."

"Would you like some water?"

"Please?"

She lifted his head and held a canteen to his mouth.
The water was tepid, but the wetness felt wonderful
on his lips and his parched throat.

"That's enough," she said, taking the canteen away.
"Can you talk?"

"I—I think so."

"Do you know where you are?"

He frowned. Hadn't he figured that out before?

"Nevada Territory?"

"Good," she said. "Now a hard question. Do you
know your name?"

"Skye Fargo."

"It is him," she said, looking up at whoever was driving the wagon.

That was it. The ground wasn't moving, he was on a moving wagon.

"How—how did I get here?"

"Here?" she asked. "You mean on the wagon?"

"Yes."

"We put you here."

"We?"

"My husband and I," she said. "I'm Karen Judd, this is my husband, Henry."

Fargo couldn't see the husband from his vantage point, so he took her word for it.

"We found you lying on the ground and put you in our wagon. We're taking you to our place—unless you have somewhere else you'd like to go?"

"No," he said, "not that I know of."

"When we get there we'll send for the doctor," Karen Judd said. "I see you've hit your head. Do you have any other injuries?"

"My—my legs."

"Which one?" She looked as if she was reaching down to his legs, but he didn't feel anything.

"Both of them."

"What's wrong? Do they hurt? They didn't seem broken."

"I . . . can't feel them."

"Oh, my," she said. "Can you feel that?"

He didn't know what she was doing, but for all the feeling he had she could have been prodding him with a hot poker.

"No."

The look of concern on her face deepened. She had red hair piled up on top of her head right now, with errant tendrils falling down over her face. Her skin was pale and flawless, and he found it odd he'd notice the light sprinkle of freckles on the bridge of her nose, even in his present condition.

She said something to him then, but he didn't hear it. He couldn't see her very well anymore, either, and before long there was that darkness again.

Fargo didn't see much of the Judd place when they arrived. He was awake but on his back when they got there, and then Henry Judd got another man to help carry him inside. Karen Judd had gone in ahead to fix up a bed for him. Fargo was very grateful that he'd been found in his helpless condition by people who were anxious to help, and not by someone who might have taken advantage of the situation to rob him, or do worse.

Still, what was there to rob him of? Apparently his horse was gone, along with his rig. The first thing he was going to have to do when he got back on his feet was find the Ovaro and get him back.

Of course, getting on his feet was going to have to come first, and right now he couldn't even move his legs, let alone stand on them.

They set him down on a bed with sheets so fresh he could smell them. The two men left, but Karen Judd stayed behind. Skye Fargo had been admiring beautiful women all his life and a little thing like having his legs paralyzed didn't stop him from admiring her. She was full-bodied, and the full thrust of her breasts was like a challenge.

Likewise, women had been casting all kinds of glances Fargo's way his whole life, and this was no different. With her husband out of the room she was studying him quite openly and unabashedly. Fargo had the impression that this was a very headstrong woman who usually got what she wanted.

"I hope I'm not putting anyone out," he said.

"Putting out—oh, you mean the bed?"

He nodded.

"Am I making somebody sleep on the floor?"

"No, no, we have our own bed, this one is an extra one," she said. "You're not putting anyone out. Put that out of your mind."

She came closer and sat on the edge of the bed.

"My husband is going for the doctor." She touched his forehead, and her hand was very warm and tender. For a moment her fingers touched his hair, and then she pulled them away, as if he'd burned her.

"Are you hungry?"

"Actually, I am," he said.

"I'll get you some soup while we wait for the doctor to arrive, and you can get some rest, too." She rose and walked to the door. "I'll leave this open so you can call me . . . if you want me."

Fargo thought for sure that she was sending him all kinds of signals. At the moment, though, he wasn't in any condition to do anything about it. He tried to lie back but he was suddenly feeling pain in his lower back. He rolled over and found that he was more comfortable when lying on his side. His head was still pounding, but the bleeding had stopped. All there was to do now was wait for the doctor and find out what was wrong with his legs.

Karen Judd returned about twenty minutes later with a steaming hot bowl of soup.

"How far away is that doctor?" Fargo asked.

"They should be back pretty soon," she said, putting the bowl on the night table next to the bed. She pulled a chair over, as well.

"What are you doing?"

"I'm going to feed you your soup."

"I think I can do that."

"Can you?" she asked. "Sit up."

He rolled onto his back, then tried to pull himself into a seated position. The pain in his lower back was too great. He turned onto his side, once again.

"Okay, you're right," he said. "I can't feed myself."

"Open wide," she said, picking up the bowl. She spooned out some soup and he opened his mouth. The soup was hot, but not so hot that it would burn him. It was also good. With the next spoonful, though, she managed to spill a little down his chin.

"Wait," she said as he reached up to wipe it.

She put the bowl down, leaned over him and licked the soup from his chin. She didn't stop there. She licked his mouth, then kissed him, hard, forcing her tongue past his lips. He reached up to cup one of her firm breasts and he could feel her hard nipple through her dress. His penis swelled, and he was happy to see that this part of his body was still working.

She continued to kiss him and ran her hand down over his body, stopping at his crotch as she felt his hardness through the sheet and blanket. She closed her hand over him as he rubbed his thumb over the hard nub of her nipple, and she moaned into his mouth, kissing him even more ardently, if that was possible.

Fargo didn't know how well he'd be able to perform

15

while unable to move his legs, but he was about to unbutton the front of her dress when they both heard the sound of a buggy pulling up in front of the house.

She pulled her mouth away from his, very unwillingly, and stood up. She stared down at him, her eyes glittering, her breathing labored.

"Another time," she said in a whisper, and left the room.

He hoped her husband could not interpret that look in her eyes. He was in no mood to handle a jealous man.

2

When Karen reentered the room, she had her husband and another man with her. She seemed to have regained control over her breathing, and her eyes were sharp and in focus. No one would have ever guessed that she had been close to devouring Fargo just moments ago.

"Mr. Fargo, I should introduce you to my husband, Henry Judd. You two didn't get a chance to meet."

Henry Judd was older than his wife, perhaps by as much as fifteen years, which put him in his late forties. He stepped forward and shook Fargo's hand. The callouses on his hand were well defined and hard.

"I appreciate what you're doing for me, Mr. Judd," Fargo said.

"Think nothing of it, Mr. Fargo. We couldn't very well leave you out there once we found you, now could we?"

"Thankfully, I suppose not."

"This is Dr. Adams," Judd said. "He's a very fine doctor."

"I'm the only one in these parts," Dr. Adams said, "so he has to say that."

Adams was in his sixties, but seemed robust enough. His blue eyes were sharp, his complexion almost pink, and while his hair was snow white it was as thick as it had probably ever been.

"I think you folks better get out, now, and allow me to examine my patient."

"I can stay and help," Karen said. "You know, like a nurse?"

"All right," Adams said. He removed his jacket and rolled up his sleeves. "You can start by getting me a basin of water and some cloths."

"Right away."

Both Karen and Henry Judd left the room. Dr. Adams leaned over Fargo and said, "Let's have a look at you."

Doc Adams gave Fargo a thorough examination, which made it necessary for him to help Fargo off with all his clothes. Lying there naked Fargo was very aware of Karen Judd examining him over the doctor's shoulder. Her eyes fell on his penis, which was no longer erect but, nonetheless, held her attention. Fargo had to look away from her at Doc Adams to make sure he didn't start to react to her, again, in the doctor's presence.

Adams cleaned the wound on Fargo's head, and turned him over when he explained about the pain in the small of his back, and his useless legs.

When he was done the doctor covered Fargo with a sheet and sat down in the chair next to the bed. Karen continued to eye Fargo hungrily, even through the sheet.

"What's the verdict, Doc?" Fargo asked.

"I'm worried about your legs."

"So am I. Is this . . . permanent?"

"Well, I think it's related to the pain in the small of your back. I believe that when you fell from your horse you landed on the small of your back. There's a bruise there, and a swelling. I think the swelling is putting pressure somewhere, rendering your legs useless."

"I guess my question is the same, Doc," Fargo said. "Is it permanent?"

"I'm afraid we won't know that until the swelling goes down," Adams said. "It's possible that when that happens you'll regain the movement in your legs."

"And if I don't?"

Dr. Adams patted him on the shoulder and said, "Why don't we cross that bridge when we come to it, Mr. Fargo. Besides, you'll probably be more interested right now in your head wound."

"Why's that?" Fargo asked.

"Because," Doc Adams said, "it wasn't caused by hitting your head when you fell."

"What caused it, Doc?" Karen asked.

"A bullet," Adams said. "Somebody blew you right out of your saddle, Mr. Fargo."

"A bullet?" Karen asked. "But who—"

"I remember a shot," Fargo said.

And, suddenly, he did. It came back to him. He heard the shot and reacted a split second too late. A man of lesser reflexes would not have reacted at all and would have been killed, but Fargo threw himself from his saddle at the sound of the shot, causing the bullet to crease his skull rather than imbedding itself in it.

"Whoever did it," Doc Adams said, "must have thought you were dead. They didn't bother to check."

"That was their first mistake," Fargo said. "Their

last was stealing my horse. They're going to pay for both."

"Well," Adams said, standing up and sweeping the tools of his trade into his black bag, "you're going to have to recover the movement in your legs, first."

"Believe me, Doctor," Fargo said, "they'll pay for both mistakes if I have to crawl."

The doctor stared at Fargo and, behind him, Karen experienced a shiver unlike anything she'd ever experienced before.

"Yes," Dr. Adams said, "I believe you—but with any luck, you won't have to crawl. Once that swelling goes down . . . well, we'll see." He turned to Karen. "Meanwhile, I'll leave him in your capable hands, Karen."

"Isn't there a hotel in town I could move to?" Fargo asked. "I don't want to be a burden—"

"You be quiet, Mr. Fargo," she said, cutting him off. "You're not going to be a burden to anyone. I'll take good care of him, Doc."

Adams turned to Fargo.

"I'd suggest you stay here, Mr. Fargo," the doctor said. "I don't want you moving about just yet."

"All right, Doctor," Fargo said, "whatever you say."

If it was fate that he stay here with Karen Judd—and her husband—then so be it. Something was certainly brewing between him and the lovely woman, and he was in no condition to avoid it—and wasn't sure he wanted to. If anything, it would be a pleasant diversion from worrying about his legs, and what he'd do if he could never move them again.

"I'll take real good care of him," Karen said to the doctor as they walked to the door.

* * *

Karen was true to her word. That night she brought him some dinner and sat there feeding it to him. There was no repeat of what had happened earlier in the day, and neither of them made reference to it.

"That was a fine meal, Mrs. Judd."

"Oh," she said, "I think you should call me Karen, since you're going to be our guest for a while."

"All right, Karen."

"And I'll call you Skye."

"That's fine."

"How about some coffee?"

"I'd like that."

But instead of bringing the coffee in herself, it was Henry Judd who brought it.

"I wanted to talk to you," Judd said. He'd brought in two cups, one for him and one for Fargo. "Mind if I sit?"

"Not at all," Fargo said. "It's your house, I'm just a guest."

"A little more than a guest, if truth be told."

Fargo, turned on one side to avoid putting pressure on the small of his back, held the coffee carefully, so as not to spill it.

"I don't understand."

"Do you remember why you were coming here, Fargo? I mean, specifically, why you were coming to this valley?"

Fargo frowned. There were still a few gaps caused by the bullet wound to his head that had not yet been filled in.

"No, I can't say that I do."

"You were coming here to work for me."

"I was?"

21

"I sent for you," Judd said, "and when you didn't arrive we went looking for you."

"Well," Fargo said, "I'm lucky you did."

"I'm not gonna bother you with the particulars, yet," the rancher said, "because obviously you ain't up to it. Later, when you get your legs back, we can talk."

"Yes," Fargo said, "when I get them back."

"Henry!"

Judd immediately got a guilty look on his face and turned to face his wife.

"You were supposed to bring Mr. Fargo his coffee, not bother him."

"He's not bothering me, Mrs. Judd," Fargo said. "We were just talking."

"I'll let you get some rest," Judd said, standing up. "We can talk another time."

"Sure," Fargo said.

As Judd slipped by his wife she looked at Fargo and said, "You finish your coffee and then get some sleep. I'll check in on you later."

"All right, Mrs.—Karen, thanks."

Left alone Fargo put the coffee on the table and then turned onto his stomach, which was a comfortable position for him. His intention had been to spend some time going over the shooting incident, to see if he could dredge up any more facts. Maybe he'd seen something, or heard something other than the shot that would be helpful. However, once he turned onto his stomach fatigue overtook him, and he fell asleep. . . .

He woke later, unsure of the time and totally unaware of where he was. He didn't like the feeling, and

22

he felt for his gun. It wasn't there, and he liked that feeling even less.

He started to sit up, but his useless legs hindered him. He found himself in a cold sweat, and when he was finally able to roll over onto his side he saw Karen sitting there, watching him. Seeing her, he remembered where he was, and relaxed a bit.

"My gun," he said.

"It's here," she said, "in a dresser drawer."

"I'd like to have it near the bed."

"Of course."

She got up, walked to the dresser, retrieved the gun and gunbelt from a drawer, and brought it to the bed.

"Shall I hang it here?" she asked, indicating the bedpost.

"Yes, please."

She did so, then sat down again in the chair next to the bed.

"What are you doing here?"

"I heard you moaning," she said. "I came in to see if I could help."

He laughed without humor and almost asked her if she could do something about his legs. Instead, he said, "I smell like a goat."

"You smell like a man."

"A dirty, sweaty man."

"Would you like a bath?"

"I couldn't make it to the tub."

"You won't need to," she said. "I'll wash you."

The idea appealed to him, but . . .

"I couldn't ask you to—"

"I'm offering."

"Your husband . . ."

23

"Is asleep," she said, "and he sleeps soundly. Besides, he wouldn't object to my bathing you."

Maybe not, Fargo thought, but what about what a bath might lead to?

"All right," he said. He needed the bath, and who knew what she needed? If the husband was asleep . . . well, what the hell.

"I'll be right back."

She left and returned with a basin of water and a washcloth.

"Your back first," she said. "Lie on your belly."

He did so and she lowered the sheet. He was still naked from the doctor's examination. She dipped the cloth in the water and began to wash his back. The water was very warm and it felt good. So did her hand beneath the cloth.

She cleaned his back then went lower and started rubbing the cloth over his buttocks. He closed his eyes and gave himself up to the sensations from the water, the cloth, her hand. She rubbed the cloth over him hard, kneading his ass cheeks, and then suddenly the cloth was gone and it was just her hands. She dipped them in the water and rubbed them over him, up and down his legs, cleaning his feet, then back up again and between his thighs, brushing his balls not so accidently.

She spent some extra time on the small of his back, using the cloth again, soaking it in hot water and holding it to the bruised area.

"That feels good," he said.

"The doctor said heat would help."

Finally, she used a towel to dry him.

24

"Would you like to try and lie on your back so I can clean you in front?"

He knew what would happen if he turned over, but with her help he did it, anyway. He settled on his back, gingerly at first, and then she said, "Wait," and put a pillow beneath him so that there was no pressure on his back.

"How's that?"

"Better."

She used the cloth again, wetting it, washing his chest, spending a long time there before moving down to his belly. She skirted his crotch to do his legs and feet, then worked her way back up. When she finally touched him there it was without benefit of the cloth, again. Wetting her hands she held his testicles gently, washing them, then took his penis in her hands and stroked it, cleaning it, causing it to swell as she held it until it was rigid and hard in her hands.

"Oh my," she said, and dipped her head. Before he knew it he was in her mouth and she was sucking him, her head bobbing up and down, one hand holding the base of his penis, the other fondling his big balls.

He started out watching the door, in case her husband came in, but soon his eyes were closed and he was concentrating only on her hot mouth as she continued to suck him avidly. She let him free from her mouth only long enough to lick the length of him, wetting him thoroughly, and then taking him back inside. She stroked him and sucked him until he could stand it no more and he exploded into her mouth with a guttural moan. She moaned, as well, as she accommodated every drop he had to give her. She released him from her mouth again, wet her hands, and washed

25

him thoroughly and was amazed when his penis did not soften.

"You're an amazing man," she said, still holding him.

"And you're an amazing woman."

"What do I do with you now?" she asked. "Look at you."

"What about what I can do for you?"

"I—I wouldn't want to hurt you. If I sat astride you it would put pressure on your back."

"Not if you didn't put all your weight on me."

Now she looked at the door, over her shoulder, and then back at Fargo. She stood up then and removed her dress. Her body glowed in the light from the lamp. Her breasts were large enough to cast shadows on her belly, and he could smell the sharp, delicious scent of her readiness.

She got onto the bed with him, straddling him. He could feel the heat coming from her body.

"Tell me if I hurt you?"

"I will."

The truth was he hardly felt her, probably because his legs were so numb. She suspended herself above him, and he noticed the play of muscles along her legs and thighs. She reached down, took hold of him, guided the spongy head of his penis to her moist portal. With a sigh she settled down on him, taking him into her inch by inch, and then she began to move up and down on his shaft, holding her weight on her legs and arms, gasping each time he slid all the way into her. Fargo was able to move his hips, and he reached for her breasts and fondled them, popping the nipples between his fingers as she rode him.

"Nnn, uhh, ohhh," she moaned, and he found himself again hoping that she was right about her husband being a sound sleeper.

"Oh, God," she said. "Oh, yes, Skye, yes, I knew it would be good, but not like this . . . oh, oh, *oh*, yessss . . ."

When her time came her entire body began to shake and it was all she could do to keep from falling down on him. Her legs trembled and finally he helped her with the weight by putting his hands beneath her arms and taking her weight. The muscles in his arms bulged, and muscles rippled along his chest and the sight of him, the smell of him, the feel of him made her think she might pass out. . . .

He held her until she slid one leg over him and was able to sit on the bed, and then she lay down beside him, her head on his shoulder, one hand playing with his penis which, remarkably, was still semierect.

"Well," she said, "at least we know one part of your body that works *very* well!"

She couldn't stay with him all night, as much as she wanted to.

"I'll have to be in bed with him when he wakes up," she said.

She got off the bed and slipped her dress back on.

"Thank you for the bath," he said.

"You probably think I'm an awful wife," she said, suddenly demure.

"It's not for me to judge."

"Henry is a wonderful man, but he's older than I am, and he doesn't . . . doesn't crave me. Do you know what I mean?"

"Of course I do, Karen."

"And I don't crave him . . . not anymore . . . not the way I've craved you since the moment I saw you, lying in the dirt by the road. Even in that condition I knew . . . I knew . . ." She reached a hand out as if to touch him, then pulled it back.

"I have to go," she said. "Do you feel better now?"

"Much better," he said, and she giggled.

"I meant from the bath, silly."

"That's what I meant, too."

"I'll make you a good breakfast in the morning," she promised.

"I'll need it," he said. "I built up a hell of an appetite tonight."

She pulled the sheet up over him, touched her hand to his chest briefly, then said, "I'll see you in the morning," and left, taking with her the basin of water.

He actually did feel better. The bath had taken care of the dirt and sticky sweat that had been clinging to him, and the sex assured him that, even without legs, he could satisfy a woman, and be satisfied.

But as wonderful as the sex had been, that would be small consolation if he didn't get his legs back.

3

True to her word—and already Fargo was discovering that Karen was, in every aspect—she appeared the next morning with a big breakfast for him. Eggs, ham, potatoes, and some biscuits. Also, coffee. This time, however, neither of them was inclined to have her feed him. She said she had to make breakfast for her husband and the men who worked for them.

"How many do you have?"

"Six."

"And what do you run here, Karen?"

"Run?"

"Horses? Cattle?"

"Oh, some of both. I really don't pay much attention to the workings of the ranch. It doesn't interest me."

"So then you wouldn't know why your husband sent for me?"

"Henry sent for you?"

"That's what he told me."

"But you don't remember?"

"I still have some blank spots caused by the bullet wound," he said, touching his head. "Everything will come back to me, though." Including, he added to himself, my legs.

"Well, no, I can't say that I do know why he sent for

you," she said, touching his shoulder, and then running her hand down his arm, "but I'm glad that he did."

"Karen, about that—"

"Can't talk now," she said, moving swiftly for the door. "Gotta run. I'll be in to check on you after breakfast is finished."

Obviously, she didn't want to talk about what had happened the night before. That was fine with him. It would keep. He was more concerned with why Henry Judd might have sent for him, and who else might know about it. Was there some opposition for Judd who might have tried to kill him before he could get here? Or was he merely bushwhacked for his horse and rig? These were the questions he needed answered before anything else.

He suddenly realized he was starving, and dug into his breakfast with vigor.

It wasn't Karen who came in after breakfast but her husband, Henry.

"Thought you might want some more coffee," he said, entering with the pot in his hand.

"Thanks," Fargo said, "I could use some."

Henry Judd poured his cup full, then put the pot down on the table"

"Feel up to talkin'?" Judd asked.

"Sure," Fargo said "I've got lots of questions about why you sent for me."

"How much do you remember? I mean, about everything."

"I'm fine about who I am, if that's what you're worried about."

"You remember that they call you the Trailsman?"

"Yes," Fargo said, "it's only the last week, maybe two, that I'm having trouble with."

"I sent word out about two weeks ago," Judd said, "and you answered right quick. I was surprised at how quick. You even told us when you'd be here, which is how come we knew when to go out lookin' for you."

"And what was the job?" Fargo asked.

"It involves a family named Layton. Do you know the name?"

"I can't say that I've ever heard it before."

"You will. Ben Layton is in line to be the first governor of this territory."

"He's a politician?"

"He's . . . well, he thinks he's God in this valley."

"Why's that?"

"Maybe because he owns more than half of it. He and his sons run roughshod over this valley, and everybody just rolls over for them."

"Roughshod. How?"

"They take what they want."

"But . . . they sound wealthy. Couldn't they buy whatever they wanted?"

"Oh, yeah, but they like it better this way."

"Why would a man like that be appointed governor?"

"Because nobody will speak out against him," Judd said. "And it's mostly his boys who do the taking. It's when they get into trouble that he uses his money to buy their way out of it."

"I see, but what I don't see is why you sent for me, or what you expected me to do about it?"

"Well, for a long time I was one of the people who just looked the other way."

"And what changed that?"

"One of Layton's sons, Tad, the middle one, decided he wanted a piece of property that was on my land. See, he's getting married, and this piece of land overlooks a small lake. It's the prettiest spot on my property."

"And you don't want to sell?"

"There was never any question of selling," Judd said. "He just wants it. He's going to build on it."

"Why don't you go to the law?"

"I told you," Judd said, "Layton owns half this valley, and that includes the sheriff."

"I don't know what I can do for you, Henry."

"There's something else you ought to know."

"Like what?"

"The youngest of the Laytons, Lonnie."

"What about him?"

"He likes horses."

"So?"

"When he sees one he likes," Judd said, "he takes it, and he doesn't care how he does it. He's taken some of mine."

Fargo tried to sit up straighter and it caused a twinge of pain in his lower back that he ignored.

"Are you saying he's the one who shot me and took my horse?"

"I'm sayin' it could be," Judd said. "It's more'n likely."

"How old is this Lonnie Layton?"

"Twenty."

"And the others?"

32

"All in their twenties," Judd said. "Tad's about twenty-five and Andy, he's the oldest, is probably twenty-eight or nine—about Karen's age.

That surprised Fargo. Karen was beautiful, but he'd guessed her age in her early thirties.

"And Ben Layton?"

"Ben's about fifty-five, but he's as robust and strong as his sons."

"And they have a spread near here?"

"Biggest in the valley."

"But this Tad, he wants your piece of land."

"It's the prettiest in the valley."

Fargo nodded, thinking about the young one, Lonnie, trying to kill him because he liked his horse. Fargo's Ovaro was a fine-looking specimen, there was no doubt. Lots of men had offered him money for the animal. To have someone try to take it from him this way was more than he could ignore.

"Henry," Fargo said, "we'll have to wait and see what happens with my legs, but when I can ride would you loan me a horse?"

"Sure," Henry said, "I've got plenty. What are you gonna do?"

"I just thought I'd ride out and pay my respects to the richest man in the valley," Fargo said, "the future governor of the territory."

Karen did not reappear until early afternoon. When she entered she saw Fargo trying to swing his legs off the bed.

"What are you trying to do?" she asked, rushing to him. "Kill yourself?"

"I just wanted to see if I could stand."

"And if you can't you'll fall over and hurt yourself."

"Just help me, Karen," he said, "or stay out of my way."

"Oh! You stubborn . . . man!" she said. "Here, lean on me."

She stood next to him so he could put his hand on her shoulder. He got his feet onto the floor but frowned, because he couldn't feel the rough wood beneath his bare skin.

"Are you all right?"

"Yes," he said, "just . . . help me up."

She put one hand around his waist and together they got him to his feet.

"You're up."

He couldn't have told that from the way it felt. It was very odd to be standing, but to be unable to feel his legs or his feet.

"All right," he said, "let me go, and move away."

"Okay," she said, and released him gently. When he didn't topple immediately she moved away from him—and he fell over backward, back onto the bed. He discovered that it is very difficult to stand when you have no feeling in your legs.

"Okay, that's enough for today," she said.

He got himself around on the bed and sat there, staring accusingly at his useless legs, ignoring the throbbing pain in his lower back.

"You can try again tomorrow," she said.

"Yes," he said, "and the day after that, and the day after that until I can stand."

"And then what?" she asked.

"And then the next step is to walk."

"The doctor said—"

"I know what the doctor said," Fargo said, "but I've

got some business to take care of with a family named Layton."

She helped him lie back on the bed and covered him with the sheet.

"Has Henry been in here talking to you, again?"

"He has."

"About the Laytons?"

"Yes."

She shook her head and sat down on the bed.

"There's something you should know, Skye."

"What's that?"

"I almost married Ben Layton," she said.

"Why didn't you?"

"I changed my mind at the last minute."

"Why?"

"Well . . . it was his oldest son, Andy."

"What did he have to do with it?"

"Everything," she said. "I was . . . I got involved with him."

"With the son of the man you were supposed to marry?"

She nodded.

"It just wouldn't have been a good idea for me to marry Ben and live in that house with him and his sons."

"So how did you come to marry Henry?"

She shrugged.

"I'm not sure. Henry was just there when I called it off with Ben."

"And how did Layton take it?"

"Not well."

"And that's why his sons are taking things of Henry's. Like horses, and a piece of land?"

"Yes."

"So Henry sent for me."

"If he says he did," she said. "He didn't check with me first."

"Well, whether your husband sent for me or not is irrelevant," Fargo said, "if it was Lonnie Layton who shot me and took my horse."

Her eyes widened.

"Is that what Henry told you?"

"He said it was a possibility," Fargo said. "Now that I realize you seem to know the family, what do you think? Is it possible?"

"Well . . . it's *possible*, yes, but how would you prove it?"

"By going to the Layton spread and seeing for myself."

"And then what?" she asked. "Would you go to the sheriff? Because I don't think you'd get much cooperation out of him."

"No," Fargo said, "I wouldn't go to the sheriff, even if he wasn't in Layton's pocket. No, this was my horse that was taken, and my *life* that was almost taken. I handle those kinds of things myself, Karen. I take them very seriously."

"If I leave you alone now do you swear you'll stay in bed?"

"Yes," Fargo said.

She was about to say something else when there was a knock on the front door.

"Who can that be?"

She left the room and went to the door. Fargo could hear the murmur of voices—hers and a man's—and then she reappeared at the door of the room.

"Skye, there's someone here to see you."

"Who? I don't know anyone around here."

"It's Sam Brannon," she said.

"Who?"

"Sheriff," she said, "Sam Brannon."

That surprised Fargo.

"The sheriff, huh?" he said. "Well, send him in, darlin', and let's see what's on his mind."

"All right . . ."

"Wait, Karen."

"Yes?" She stepped into the room.

"What did you tell him about my injury?" Fargo asked in a low voice.

"Nothing."

"Good," he said, "let me handle it. I don't want him to know about my legs."

She nodded her understanding and went to fetch the lawman.

4

When Sheriff Sam Brannon entered the room he did so slowly, almost laconically. Fargo knew the man knew who he was—otherwise why would he be here?—and he was trying to show that it didn't impress him.

He was tall and real slender, probably somewhere in his thirties.

"Skye Fargo?"

"That's right."

"I'm Sam Brannon." The man actually tapped the star on his chest. "Sheriff."

"I can see that."

"Laid up, huh?"

"For a little while."

"Serious?"

"Scalp wound," Fargo said. "Somebody took a shot at me."

"That's what I heard," Brannon said. "Thought I'd come out and see if it was really true that somebody outgunned the Trailsman."

Fargo laughed.

"I'd hardly say someone outgunned me, Sheriff," he replied, "unless you count being bushwhacked by some coward being outgunned."

"I wouldn't let that kind of talk get around."

"Why not?" Fargo asked. "Are you saying you know who the coward was who shot me, and he wouldn't like being called a coward?"

"No," Brannon said quickly, "I didn't say that at all. How would I know who shot you?"

"I don't know, Sheriff," Fargo said. "I don't know how well you do your job."

"I do okay."

"So now that you've seen me, now what?"

"Just doin' my job, Fargo," Brannon said. "How long you intend to be around?"

"The doctor says I should stay in bed a few days."

"For a scalp wound?"

"I'm having some dizziness," Fargo said. "He just wants to be cautious."

Brannon's eyes fell on Fargo's gun hanging on the bedpost.

"See you keep your iron handy."

"You never know, do you?"

"No, I, uh, guess you never do. Guess I'll be goin', then. I just thought I'd, uh, drop by."

Fargo felt sure the lawman had been told to drop by. Word must have gotten around that the Trailsman wasn't dead, like somebody thought.

"Tell me something, Sheriff," Fargo said as the man headed for the door.

"What's that?"

"How'd you happen to know I was here?"

"Word just, uh, ya know, gets around."

"I see."

"Well, I'll get goin'."

"When I'm up and around," Fargo said, "I'll come and see you."

39

The sheriff froze for a moment, as if this was a threat.

"Oh, uh, sure," he said, and went out the door.

It was only seconds later when Karen came back into the room.

"Tell me about Sam Brannon, Karen."

"Not much to tell. He was just about appointed to the job by Ben Layton."

"Is he any good at it?"

"What'd you think?"

"I think he pretty much does what he's told to do."

"You're right about that."

"Which means he was told to come here and see how badly hurt I am."

"By Ben Layton?"

"He does the telling around here, doesn't he?"

"Pretty much."

"There's another question here, too."

"What's that?"

"How'd they know I was here?"

"Maybe one of our hands talked in town."

"Maybe."

"I didn't say anything."

"What about Henry?" Fargo asked. "Would he have passed the word?"

"Why would he?"

Fargo shrugged.

"Maybe he just wanted people to know that the Trailsman was at his house."

"What would that accomplish?"

"I don't know," Fargo said. "I guess I'll have to ask him about it. Tell me something about Henry, Karen."

"Like what?"

"Like what kind of man he is?"

Karen clasped her hands in front of her, looking oddly demure to Fargo.

"I suppose he's not the man I thought he was."

"And what kind of man did you think he was?" Fargo asked.

"Strong, brave, dependable."

"Is he any of those things?"

"No," she said, "I'm afraid he isn't. And I'm afraid he doesn't satisfy me, or fulfill . . . me in any way."

"Why do you stay, then?"

"We're married."

That didn't seem to bother her when she was naked and in bed with Fargo, but he didn't comment on that. She did, however, as if she were reading his mind.

"I know what you're thinking," she said. "I'll have sex with another man behind my husband's back, but I won't leave him."

That was almost right. He was thinking that she had no problem having sex with another man *right under her husband's nose*!

"It's not for me to judge you, Karen," Fargo said. "You have to do whatever's right for you." Suddenly, he was hit by a twinge of pain . . . in his leg!

"What is it?"

"I felt something . . . in my left leg."

"That's wonderful."

He concentrated for a few moments, trying to move his legs, but ended up drenched in perspiration.

"Don't force it, Skye," Karen said. "Your legs will come back to you."

"They better," he said. "I have a lot of work for them to do."

41

"And I have a lot of work to do, too," she said. "I'll let you rest."

"Where is Henry, Karen?"

"He's out working. Should I tell him the sheriff was here when he comes home?"

"Yes," Fargo said, "and after that I'll talk to him. If he's passing around the word that I'm here to help him, while I'm in this condition, he could end up getting me killed . . . and I wouldn't like that, at all!"

Fargo heard Henry Judd arrive home and waited for Karen to give him the news about the sheriff. Henry Judd appeared about ten minutes later, drying his hands on a towel.

"Karen said you wanted to talk to me," he said. "I had to clean up, first."

"Sheriff Brannon was here today, Henry."

"Karen mentioned that."

"He wanted to find out why I was here," Fargo said. "What I want to know is, how did he know I was here?

Henry didn't answer. He continued to dry his hands on the towel.

"I think your hands are dry, Henry."

"Oh, yeah . . ." the man said, holding the towel in one hand now.

"Did you tell him, Henry?"

"I might have."

"*Did* you?"

"Well . . . yeah . . ." Fargo didn't like the man much in that moment. For one thing, he didn't like grown men who acted like scolded schoolboys. For another, it was a damned stupid thing for him to have done.

"Are you trying to get me killed?"

"Of course not—"

"If Layton hears that I can't move my legs he'll pick me off clean while I'm lying here," Fargo said. "Did you tell anyone about my condition?"

"No, of course not."

"Why did you tell the sheriff I was here?"

"I just . . . wanted Layton to know that there was someone here in the valley he couldn't control."

"Well, don't mention it to anyone else, Henry, not until I can walk again."

"I won't—"

"Just don't say anything, all right?"

"All right. How are your legs, by the way? When I was in town the doctor was asking me."

"The doctor," Fargo said, shaking his head. "Damn it, I forgot about him. Will he tell anyone about my legs?"

"He doesn't usually talk about his patients."

"What about to Ben Layton?"

"Doc doesn't like Layton much, Fargo," Henry said. "I don't think he'd talk to him about you."

"Next time you see the doctor would you specifically ask him not to?"

"Sure," Henry said, "sure, I'll do that. In fact, I'll talk to him tomorrow."

"That's fine."

"Fargo, I'm real sorry—"

"Don't apologize, Henry," Fargo said, cutting the man off, "just don't make any mistakes after today."

"Okay," Henry said, "I won't. Uh, I gotta go, Karen's gettin' supper on the table."

"Go ahead, then," Fargo said. He was annoyed that the man thought he had to ask permission. Suddenly,

43

he could understand how Karen could be disappointed in her husband. He really wasn't the kind of man who could hold a woman through strength, either physical, or of character. Henry Judd was not a man Skye Fargo would ever respect or be friends with.

In fact, he wasn't even sure he wanted to work for him.

When Karen brought Fargo's dinner in she asked about his talk with Henry.

"He wouldn't tell me anything," she said, "but he pouted like a schoolboy all through dinner."

"He acted like a schoolboy, like I was scolding him," Fargo said.

"Then you know what I mean about him."

"I'm not here to pass judgment on you or your husband, Karen," the Trailsman explained, "and certainly not on your marriage."

"Are you going to work for Henry . . . when you can walk?"

"I guess I'll have to," he said. "After all, you and he pretty much saved my life."

She sat down in the chair next to the bed.

"I had to force him, you know."

"What? Force him to do what?"

"To put you in the wagon and bring you here."

"But why?" Fargo asked. "If he sent for me, why wouldn't he help me when I was hurt?"

"I don't know," she said. "He wanted to leave you there and go to town for help. I told him we couldn't do that. You might die, or whoever shot you might come back. He finally agreed, but he was worried the whole time."

44

Fargo didn't understand how Henry Judd could even consider leaving him when they found him, in his condition. Even if the man hadn't sent for him, it just wasn't the thing you did to another human being in need of help, let alone a man you expected to work for you.

Unless Henry had lied and was not the one who had sent for him, at all.

"Fargo?"

"Hmm? Oh, sorry. Did you say something?"

"Have you remembered yet that Henry did send for you?"

Fargo frowned.

"No, I don't. Are you saying maybe he didn't?"

She shrugged and said, "I don't know what I'm saying. Henry's been acting very strange lately, that's all."

She stood up to leave.

"Have you experienced any more, uh, pain in your legs?"

"Not pain, exactly," he said, "just . . . twinges, almost like a tickle."

"Well, anything is a good sign," she said. "The doctor said he'd be back in a few days. Maybe he'll be here tomorrow."

"Yeah," Fargo said, "maybe he will." Fargo considered sending for the doctor, to make sure he didn't talk to anyone about his injury, but he decided to wait and see if the man did show up tomorrow.

After Karen left, Fargo threw back the sheets and swung his legs around so that his feet touched the floor. He closed his eyes and tried to wiggle his toes. Suddenly, he felt something. When he opened his eyes and looked down his toes were moving. He also thought he could feel the wooden floor beneath his bare feet.

He did not know it until that moment, but he had been holding his breath all this time and now that he had visible proof that his legs were coming back to him, he let it out. Now he could concentrate on what he was going to do to get the Ovaro back, and to teach the person or persons who took him the error of their ways—no matter what family they belonged to.

Now the only other thing he needed was for his recent memory to return, so he could remember who, indeed, his prospective employer was to be when he came to this valley.

5

The doctor appeared not the next day but the following one, and examined Fargo. During that time Fargo came to a decision.

"Can you feel this?" he asked, prodding Fargo's left leg.

"No," Fargo lied.

"What about this?" He prodded the right leg with the same sharp instrument.

"No," Fargo lied.

"Now?"

He poked harder and Fargo managed to keep the pain from showing on his face.

"No."

The doctor looked exasperated.

"I don't understand," he said. "The swelling in the small of your back has gone down. You should start to get the feeling back in your legs—unless there's some other cause."

"Like what?"

The doctor shrugged and said, "I don't know. I'm just an old country doctor. You might need somebody better than me to examine you."

"There is no one else."

The physician closed his bag.

"I'll come back in a couple of days and we'll try again. If you don't have any feeling by then you'll have to decide what to do."

"What are my options?"

"Get another doctor to come here," the man said, "or go to another doctor."

"Tell me something, Doc."

"What's that?"

"Have you told anyone about my condition?"

"No," he said, "why should I?"

"Ben Layton, maybe. I hear he pulls a lot of strings in town."

The doctor stiffened his back and said, "Ben Layton doesn't pull my strings, Mr. Fargo!"

"Well, that's good to hear."

"Have you gotten yourself involved with him and his family?" the doctor asked. "They're a rough bunch."

"I don't know the answer to that question, yet, Doc," Fargo said.

"You're worried they'll find out you can't walk and come for you?"

"Something like that."

"Well, they're not gonna find it out from me."

"I appreciate that, Doc."

The doctor picked up his bag.

"I'll see you in a couple of days."

"I'll be here."

"Yes," the doctor said, "I imagine you will be."

The doctor left the room and Fargo swung his feet to the floor and stood up. It was only the second time he'd stood, the first being the night before. All day the day before his legs had tingled, the feeling coming

48

back into them and then that night he stood for the first time and hobbled around the room. He was still unsteady, but able to move around. He walked slowly to the window that looked out onto the front of the house and watched the doctor climb his buggy and drive off. Karen had walked him out and watched him go, as well.

Once the feeling had returned to his legs he decided not to tell anyone, not even the doctor. This would be a hole card he would use if the need arose. Meanwhile, he was waiting until he could remember who had sent for him. Once that memory came back, he'd be whole again. At that time he'd head out to get his horse, saddle and rifle back, as well as the belongings that were in his saddlebags.

As Karen turned and walked back into the house he walked slowly back to the bed and got into it.

Karen had come to him again in the night and climbed into bed with him. It was all he could do during sex not to move his legs—but then again, she probably wouldn't have noticed. During sex she closed her eyes and gave herself over completely to the sensations—sensations she had been missing for a long time, since she had married her husband.

During the night he had awakened to find her hovering over him.

"What do you have in mind?" he asked.

"This," she said, and straddled him, but instead of straddling his crotch she was tantalizingly close to his face.

"We can do this," he said, and took hold of her buttocks, burying his face in her. His tongue and lips worked avidly on her and she became gushingly wet.

She kept her weight on her legs and arms, rubbing her wet slit against his face and mouth, biting her lips to keep from crying out. He found her stiff little nub and flicked it with his tongue, and if they had been in a hotel or anywhere else she would have screamed.

"Oh, God," she whispered, "it's so good, yes, yes, Fargo, right there . . . oh, oh . . . ooh, ooh . . . there . . . there . . . there!"

He felt her entire body go taut, and if he hadn't been holding tightly to her buttocks she would have come down on his chest because her legs couldn't hold her any longer. Fargo was strong enough to hold her weight until she was able to roll off of him.

"God," she said, "I don't think I can walk back to my own room."

But she did, and Fargo went to sleep with the sweet smell of her all over him. . . .

He got to the bed just in time because she came walking into the room then.

"What did he say?"

"No progress. He'll be back in a few days."

"What about the tingling you talked about?"

He shrugged and said, "It stopped."

"I'm so sorry," she said, sitting on the edge of the bed. She put her hand on his chest. "It's been so good being with you I can't wait until you get the feeling back in your legs. I want you on top of me, in me . . ." She ran her hand down his body until it rested on his penis, which was swelling just in response to her words. . . .

"Karen!"

It was Henry Judd's voice, bellowing as he came into the house.

"Damn him," she whispered, and hurried from the room.

Fargo got out of bed again and walked slowly to the door. He knew he was going to have to start moving around more, exercising his legs. They were weak from not being used and he had to get them in shape again for walking, and for riding . . . as well as for other things. . . .

He peered out the door and watched as Henry and Karen Judd talked.

"I need you to cook for the men."

"What about the cook?"

"He quit."

"What? Why?"

"He hired on with Layton's outfit."

"He's not that good a cook, Henry. Layton only wanted to hire him away from you."

"Don't you think I know that?"

"You'll have to go to town and get a new cook," she said. "I'm not going to start cooking for six men."

"Five."

"What?"

"Del Winter quit," he said.

"To work for Layton?"

"No," Henry said, "he just . . . quit. Said he didn't think we'd be needing all these men much longer."

"God," she said, "even the men can see the end coming."

"The end is *not* coming!"

"It's time to sell, Henry."

"I'm not selling my ranch, Karen."

"Why not?" she demanded. "Isn't it better to sell it than have him take it piece by piece?"

"He's not gonna take it."

"And are you going to stop him?"

"No," Henry said, "Fargo is."

"Fargo can't walk," she said, "or haven't you noticed?"

"He'll walk, soon."

"What if he doesn't?" she asked. "What if he never walks again?"

"Would that matter to you?" he asked. "You could still go to his bed and rut with him, couldn't you? Wouldn't you like that? To keep him here forever so he can satisfy you?"

Fargo saw Karen's hands go to her mouth and her face turn red.

"Do you think I'm a fool? That I don't know what's going on?"

"And you haven't said anything?"

"Why should I?"

"You could put him out of the house. If you were man you'd do that."

"Right now," Henry said, "I need Fargo a lot more than I need a wife."

That shocked Karen into silence.

"You prepare dinner for the men," he said. "Afterward I'll go into town and see if I can hire a cook."

He stormed out of the house then and she stood in the middle of the kitchen, her face buried in her hands. Fargo turned and went back to the bed, feeling as if he had intruded on their conversation.

So Henry knew about him and Karen. Fargo decided right there and then that it would soon be time

52

for him to leave, probably another couple of days. He couldn't stay in this house much longer—and he had things to do. He'd spent more time in a bed these past few days than he ever had. He was even starting to miss sleeping on the hard ground.

He was going to have very little tolerance for whoever shot him and stole his horse. He didn't care whose son it was, they were probably going to end up *under* the hard ground.

6

Karen didn't come to his room that night, or the night after. That suited him. He loved women and he, too, was looking forward to being in bed with her when all his parts worked, even his legs. But now that her husband knew what was going on, it changed things—especially for her.

He continued to exercise his legs, walking around the room whenever he was alone. The night before the doctor was to return he was feeling almost normal, except for a slight ache that persisted in his back.

He was sleeping lighter, too. He couldn't depend on Henry Judd to keep his mouth shut. Just at the right—or wrong—time Henry might decide he wanted Fargo dead for sleeping with his wife. He might pass the word on about Fargo's "condition," and that could bring someone crawling to a window at night to put a bullet in him while he slept. Whatever Henry's beef with the Laytons was, the husband in him might suddenly decide he had a bigger beef with Skye Fargo.

So Fargo slept lightly, which was why he heard something outside, the scrape of a foot perhaps. He was off the bed by the time the shot was fired. He grabbed his own gun from the holster on the bedpost and fired back at the window. He heard the cry of a man and the thud of a bullet as it plowed through flesh and bone.

He was out the bedroom door and heading for the front when Karen and Henry Judd came from their room.

"Fargo!" Henry yelled.

"Skye!" Karen said in surprise.

He didn't answer either of them, or stop. He was out the door, wearing only his underwear. When he got to the window there was a man lying under it, a gun in the dirt beside him. Fargo kicked the gun away and then leaned over and checked the man.

"Is he dead?" Henry asked from behind him.

"Yes."

Fargo straightened and faced Henry.

"Do you know him?"

"It's dark," Henry said, "I can't see his face."

Karen appeared then, carrying a lighted lamp. Fargo took it from her and held it to the man's face, which gave it a yellow glow, but illuminated it.

"Do you know him?" Fargo asked. "Either of you?"

Both peered at the man's face and shook their heads.

"No," Henry said, "I don't know him."

"Neither do I."

Fargo put the lamp down on the ground and went through the man's pockets, coming up empty.

"Fargo," Karen said, "when did you start walking?"

"A couple of nights ago."

"And you didn't tell us?" Henry asked.

"You continued to let me wait on you?" Karen asked.

Fargo straightened up again, handing Karen back the lamp.

"I didn't want anyone to know."

He walked past them back to the house. Some of the hands came running up to see what the commotion was.

"Get this body into the barn, boys," Henry Judd called out, "and see if any of you know him."

Henry and Karen followed Fargo into the house. When he reached the bedroom he was pulling on his trousers. It was good to have them on again.

"Why didn't you tell us?" Karen asked. "Didn't you trust us?"

"No," Fargo said, "I didn't trust anyone, and I didn't want anyone to know. I thought something like this might happen, and I wanted whoever it was who showed up to get careless."

"And he did," Henry said.

"Henry," Fargo said, strapping on his gunbelt, "you better send someone for the sheriff."

"Right."

"Karen," he said, "make some coffee, will you?"

"Make your own damn coffee!" she snapped, and stalked out of the room.

Fargo put his shirt on and buttoned it.

"Henry," he said, "do you have a horse I can use?"

"Where are you going?" Henry asked. "Aren't you gonna wait for the sheriff?"

"I'll be back," Fargo said. "I want to go and talk to Ben Layton before word gets out about this."

"You think this is one of Layton's men?"

"I don't know," Fargo said, "but if it is, I want to be the one to tell him that he's dead. Now, about that horse . . ."

*   *   *

Following directions given by Henry, Fargo rode to the Layton ranch. Feeling a horse beneath him again was like being born again. The elation he felt surprised even him. Even the ache in the small of his back couldn't do anything to diminish it. He was on a horse again, and whole again. Now all he needed was to get his own horse back.

When he reached the Layton house it was impressive. Two floors, and they were all lit up. As he approached it several men got between him and the house.

"Can we help you?" one of them asked.

"I'd like to see Mr. Layton."

"And who are you?"

"My name's Skye Fargo," Fargo said, and in a sudden flash of memory he remembered something. "He sent for me."

Fargo was admitted to the house and taken to the "library" to wait for Ben Layton. When the doors opened, however, it was not Ben Layton who entered, but a girl—a young woman, really, of about twenty-two or -three.

"Hello," she said.

She was lovely, tall, and slender, with small, high breasts with the shape and firmness of peaches. Her clothes were tight, but they were man's clothes, shirt and jeans, and they showed off her body.

"Hello."

"Are you Mr. Fargo?"

"That's right."

"My father sent me down to look after you," she said. "He'll be down in a few minutes."

"Your father?"

"I'm Andrea Layton," she said, and came forward to shake his hand. Her grip was firm, the handshake brief.

"Is something wrong?" she asked.

"No, nothing," Fargo said, "I just didn't know there was a Layton daughter."

"That's because all anyone ever talks about are the Layton sons."

"Now that I see you," Fargo said, "I know that's very foolish of them."

She laughed and said, "I see you know how to talk to women, Mr. Fargo. I'm going to have to watch out for you."

At that moment the doors opened again and a thickset man entered, wearing a pair of trousers and a silk smoking jacket. His hair was carefully combed and still wet, his cheeks appeared to have been recently shaved.

"Mr. Fargo?"

"Yes, Father, this is the infamous Skye Fargo, otherwise known as the Trailsman."

Layton came forward, hand extended. He gave Fargo what he now recognized as the Layton handshake, firm but brief.

"We didn't expect you to arrive quite this late."

"Late as in the hour?" Fargo asked. "Or are we talking days?"

"Well, you are several days later than you said you'd be."

"Actually," Fargo said, "I arrived on time, but I was . . . waylaid."

"Waylaid?"

"Ambushed might be a better word," Fargo said. "I was shot, and my horse was stolen."

"That's terrible," Andrea Layton said.

"Where have you been all this time?"

"I thought you might have known," Fargo said. "I've been at the Judd place."

"What the hell were you doing at Henry Judd's?" Layton demanded.

"He and his wife found me, and nursed me until I could get . . . back on my feet."

"Karen," Layton said, and a pained look crossed his face. He turned away, as if to hide it.

"Mr. Fargo," Andrea said, "could I offer you a drink? Brandy, perhaps?"

"That would be nice."

"Father?"

"Hmm?"

"Brandy?"

"Oh, yes, my dear," Layton said, turning back to face Fargo. "Won't you have a seat?"

Actually, sitting down sounded like a good idea. His back was really aching from the ride over. He accepted a snifter of brandy from Andrea and sat down on a plush sofa in the middle of the room. Andrea sat at the opposite end of it, and Layton sat in a matching armchair.

"I thought word had gotten around that I was at the Judds'," Fargo said.

"What made you think that?" Layton asked.

"Well, the doctor was out there, and the sheriff."

"I didn't hear anything about it, but then I haven't been to town in the past week. What about you, my dear? Did you hear anything?"

"No, Father," she said, "not a word."

The two of them had such looks of innocence on their faces that Fargo instinctively knew they were lying.

"Well, somebody knew, because a man came out to the Judd place tonight to see me."

"See you?"

"He tried to kill me."

"Oh, my," Andrea said. "And what happened?"

"I killed him, instead."

"So you don't know who he was," Layton said, "or who sent him?"

"That's right."

"It's too bad you couldn't have taken him alive, then."

"I didn't have the choice."

"Well, why did you decide to come out and see us so late tonight?" Andrea asked.

"Just to bring you the news that I was here," Fargo said, "and alive."

"And ready to go to work?" Layton asked.

"Well, not quite," Fargo said.

"What do you mean?" Layton asked. "You did agree to work for me. We worked all the details out in the mail."

"There is the little matter of finding out who shot me, and stole my horse, and planting him in the ground."

"You intend to kill the person who stole your horse?" Andrea asked, as if this were a wild notion.

"Oh, yes," Fargo said. "You see, when someone tries to kill me I take it very personally."

"But what about my problem?" Layton asked.

The truth of the matter was that while Fargo had suddenly remembered that it was Ben Layton he had been coming to this valley to work for, he still didn't know why.

"I guess it'll have to wait until I solve my problem," Fargo said. He stood up. "By the way, where are your sons?"

"I don't know, actually," Layton said, also standing. "Still in town, I suppose. If they were home I would have brought them in to meet you."

"That's okay," Fargo said, "I'll meet them another time."

"Are you leaving?" Andrea asked.

"I have to," Fargo said. "The sheriff is going to want to talk to me about the man I killed. Maybe he'll even recognize him."

"Maybe he will," Layton said. "After all, that's part of his job, isn't it? Recognizing the undesirables who come to town."

"Yes, it is," Fargo said. "Thank you for the brandy, Miss Layton, and the hospitality."

"You'll come back, of course," Andrea said. "I mean, after you've solved your little problem?"

"Oh, yes," Fargo said, "I'll come back . . . maybe sooner than any of us think."

He left them to ponder that statement.

During the ride back to the Judd place Fargo thought about Ben and Andrea Layton. The father seemed to rely heavily on his daughter, which seemed odd, since he had heard nothing about her before meeting her. He wondered why neither Henry nor

Karen Judd had mentioned that there was an Andrea Layton.

When he arrived back at the Judd ranch the sheriff was waiting for him. Sheriff Brannon approached him as he limped to the house from the barn.

"You can't just kill a man and then leave," Brannon said.

"I'm back, isn't that enough? Do you know who the dead man is?"

"No," Brannon said, "I didn't recognize him."

Liar, Fargo thought.

He entered the house, the sheriff right on his heels. Henry and Karen were sitting at the kitchen table. Apparently, that's all they were doing, sitting, not talking to each other.

"Henry," Fargo asked, "did any of your men recognize the dead man?"

"No, none of them did," Henry said.

"Too bad."

"Where did you go?" Brannon asked.

Fargo turned to face him.

"I went to see Ben Layton."

Brannon's eyes widened.

"Why would you want to bother Mr. Layton this late at night?"

"Well, I had to let him know I was here," Fargo said. "After all, it was him who hired me to come."

He didn't turn, but he heard a sharp intake of breath, presumably from Karen.

"Are you going back to town, Sheriff?"

"Well, yeah, I am."

"Would you wait for me? I'd like to ride along."

"Uh, sure, okay. You're coming to town?"

"You're leaving?" Karen asked.

"Yes," he said, answering both of them. "It's time for me to get a hotel room. Wouldn't you agree, Henry?"

"Uh, oh, yeah, sure, I would," Henry said. "Time for you to be moving on."

"Not very far, though," Fargo said. "Just to town."

"You'll be, uh, staying on?" Brannon asked.

"Just until I find out who shot me, and took my horse," Fargo said. "Once I've done that, and gotten my horse back, I'll be moving on."

"I thought you were going to work for Mr. Layton?"

"No, I don't think so," Fargo said. "I don't think I really want to work for anyone around here. I'm ready to head to town when you are, Sheriff."

7

The town was called Crystal City, and it was like a lot of mining towns, only bigger. The strike in the new Nevada Territory had been a major one, and the size of the town attested to that. It appeared to have half a dozen saloons, and as many hotels, as well as all the usual stores. The streets were packed with people and he knew that the nights, after the miners were done with their day's work, would find the town even busier.

Fargo checked into the hotel late and collapsed on the bed. He'd thought that he'd never want to see another bed, but after being in the saddle so much so soon after his recovery, his back was killing him.

When he awoke the next morning he had a moment of panic. He couldn't move his legs. The condition had returned but for how long. He rolled over, trying to get his legs over the bed and his feet to the floor. They struck the floor with a thud, jarring him and seeming to bring the feeling back into his legs. He waited a moment then stood up and walked about unsteadily until his legs were completely back.

Time to go and see Dr. Adams.

* * *

"Well," Adams said, "I'm miffed that you didn't tell me the feeling was back in your legs."

"I was just being cautious, Doctor."

"I told you I wouldn't talk to anyone about your condition."

"I realize that."

"Well, never mind," Adams said. "Here's what I think happened this morning. You overdid it last night, spending too much time on horseback too soon, and you aggravated the injury."

"So this could happen again?"

"Certainly."

"For how long?"

"It may come and go until the injury completely heals."

"So I could be right in the middle of something and lose the feelings in my legs again?"

"In the middle of something? Like a gun battle? Yes, I'd say the chances were very good that it could happen again, at a moment's notice, without warning."

"Great."

"You need to give it time to heal completely, Mr. Fargo."

"I don't think I have time for that right now, Doctor," Fargo said.

"Well, it's up to you."

"Thanks for your time."

Fargo headed for the door to the doctor's office.

"Come and see me anytime while you're in town," Adams said.

"I will, Doc," Fargo said. "Thanks again."

He left the doctor's office and went to the nearest saloon.

*   *   *

Over a beer at a corner table of an empty saloon Fargo considered his options. He could lie around and wait for his injury to fully heal, so it wouldn't rear its ugly head at the wrong time. The doctor didn't know how long that would take, and Fargo didn't relish staying in Crystal City any longer than he had to. He wanted to find his horse, and the man who stole it, and get out.

According to Karen it was probably a Layton who had done it, but why would one of Ben Layton's sons ambush the man he'd hired . . . to do what?

It occurred to Fargo then that it might serve him well to find out what the job was. Maybe that would give him a hint as to why his prospective employer's son would ambush him. It would also allow him access to the grounds, and the chance to get close to the three sons—and he wouldn't mind getting closer to the daughter, in a different way. The vision of Andrea Layton in those tight trousers would not leave his mind.

That was it, then. He'd tell Layton that he was ready to take on the job, whatever the job was. That meant getting back on a horse and riding out there, and he wasn't ready to do that today. He'd stay around town today, rest his back, and get on a horse again tomorrow.

And then another way presented itself in the person of Andrea Layton—tight trousers and all—who had just entered the saloon.

"Miss Layton," the bartender said, "you know you shouldn't be in here."

"Don't worry, Dave, I'm leaving. Have you seen any of my brothers? None of them came home last night."

Dave the bartender rubbed his jaw.

"Andy was in a poker game. I don't think they wanted to stop when I closed, so they might have continued somewhere else."

"An all-night poker game," she said. "That sounds like my older brother. What about Lonnie?"

"Lonnie was drunk and talkin' to some of the girls. I think maybe they took him upstairs."

"Lonnie and some girls," she said. "Yep, that's little brother. Now what about Tad?"

"Don't know that I saw Tad last night, Miss Layton. Now could you git out of here before your pa hears I let you in here and skins me alive?"

She laughed and said, "Sure, Dave—" but as she turned she saw Fargo sitting in the corner and stopped short. "Well, now, Mr. Fargo."

"Miss Layton."

"Dave, you don't have to worry 'cause I'm not unescorted, anymore. I'll have a beer."

"Miss Layton—"

"Don't worry about it so, Dave," she said. "Just give me a beer."

She was dressed much the way she had been when he met her the night before, a man's shirt and tight trousers. Her rump looked like it wanted to burst right out of them. As she came walking over with her beer he would have sworn she was arching her back so that her breasts stuck out some more.

"Mind if I sit?" she asked.

"I don't mind at all."

She sat across from him and regarded him with obvious relish. He half expected her to lick her lips.

"You're a big man," she said. "I like big men."

"And I like pretty women."

"And you think I qualify?"

"Miss Layton," Fargo said, "you're obviously a woman who likes to play games. You *know* you're pretty. In fact, you're quite beautiful."

"I was right about you last night," she said. "You know how to talk to women."

"Aren't you supposed to be looking for your brothers?" Fargo asked. "Is that what your father sent you to town to do?"

"I've been the mother hen since Mother died," she said. "I often go out to bring the boys home."

"And how long has it been that way?"

"Since I was thirteen."

"Why do I get the feeling that the Layton boys get all the attention, but you're the one with the brains?"

She smiled.

"That's because you're a smart man—and as a smart man, have you decided to work for my father, after all?"

"As a matter of fact," he said, "I have."

She looked surprised, and then pleased.

"Well, that's wonderful."

"I was going to ride out tomorrow and tell him, but if you'd be so kind you could tell him for me."

"I'll do that, but why tomorrow?"

He gave her a smile and said, "After my injury I'm kind of sore from being back in the saddle."

"What part of you is sore?" she asked. "Maybe I can help you."

"Miss Layton—"

"Andrea."

"Andrea, a girl could get into trouble asking a man questions like that."

"I can handle trouble, Mr. Fargo—or can I call you Skye?"

"Why not?"

"I think people who go to bed together should be on a first-name basis."

"Are we going to bed together?" he asked.

"Yes, we are," she said. "I've known that ever since last night, haven't you?"

"I'd never presume such a thing upon first meeting, Andrea."

"Of course not."

"And when is this going to take place?" he asked.

"I'm not sure," she said, standing up. "I only know it's not going to be now, because I have to find those brothers of mine."

"And would your father approve of this?"

"Probably not," she said, "but then I don't always look for my father's approval before doing something."

Before she could say anything else there was a shout from an upstairs room, and then a door slammed open. A man shouted, "Yahoo!" at the top of his lungs and came running down the stairs, carrying his hat. He was about twenty-two and obviously very happy about something. He was moving so fast that he almost fell down the last half of the stairway. His shirt was not quite tucked in, and his gunbelt appeared to be on backward.

"That's my brother, Lonnie," she said. "Excuse me, Skye. We'll have to continue this another time."

"I'll be at your disposal, Andrea."

She smiled at him and said, "That's what I'm counting on."

"Dave, lemme have a beer!" Lonnie Layton said, leaning on the bar.

"No more beer for you, little brother," Andrea said, coming up next to him.

"Andrea! My big sister."

"Sometimes I think you're still fifteen years old inside, Lonnie."

"Well, sister dear, some of us don't want to grow up too fast."

"Pa sent me to bring you home, you and Tad and Andy."

"Andy's playin' poker over at Will Hutching's with some of the boys."

"Well then, let's go over and get him. Do you know where Tad is?"

"I don't remember seeing Tad since early last night," Lonnie said.

"Well, we'll have to find him, too."

"Hold that beer for me, Dave," Lonnie said, and then noticed Fargo sitting there. "Who's that?"

Andrea grabbed his arm and propelled him toward the door, saying, "I'll tell you on the way."

She tossed Fargo a smile and then they were out the door.

"That's some family," Fargo said.

"They're a wild bunch, all right," the bartender said. "You gonna be workin' for Ben Layton, mister?"

"Looks like it."

"If I was you I'd watch out for that one."

"Lonnie?"

"I ain't talkin' about Lonnie, I'm talkin' about Miss Andrea. That one's a hellion."

"Thanks for the advice," Fargo said, wondering if the man had heard all of their conversation. "I'll keep it in mind."

Fargo stood up and walked to the bar. While the bartender appeared to be talkative he figured he might as well take advantage of it.

"The way I hear it, it's the boys who were the wild ones."

"Don't you believe it," Dave said. "Although she does pretty much keep them in line she can be wilder than the three of them put together."

"Layton must be pretty proud of her."

"I don't know about that," Dave said. "The old man pretty much acts like the cock of the walk because of his three sons."

"She doesn't get any credit, huh?"

"Not much. Folks around here, though, they pretty much know who runs the house, and those three boys."

"But Ben runs the whole family, huh?"

"You said it," the bartender said. "Rules it with an iron hand. What all are you gonna be doin' for him?"

Fargo put his empty beer mug on the bar and said, "I really don't know, yet. I expect I'll be finding out to-morrow. What do I owe you?"

"Since you're gonna be around here awhile and workin' for the Laytons, I guess you'll be drinkin' on their tab," the man said. He stuck his hand out then. "Name's Dave Wilson."

"Dave," Fargo said, shaking the man's hand, "my name's Fargo."

"Nice to meetcha, Mr. Fargo."

"Just Fargo."

"You come in again, you hear, Fargo?"

"I'll be in, Dave," Fargo said. "Thanks for the beer, and the warning about Miss Andrea."

"That one's trouble, all right."

"Maybe," Fargo said, "but looking at her, I'd say she's probably not more trouble than she's worth."

"I heard that," Dave said, and gave Fargo a conspiratorial wink.

Fargo went out the batwing doors onto the street and stopped. He looked both ways, checked out the buildings across the street from the rooftops down. He decided to go over to the sheriff's office to see if the lawman had managed to find out who he had killed last night.

8

When Fargo entered the sheriff's office the man was sitting back in his chair with his feet on his desk. When he saw the Trailsman he brought his feet to the floor with a loud thump.

"Fargo. What can I do for you?"

"I was just wondering, Sheriff, if you managed to find out who that man was that I killed last night."

"Uh, no, no, I haven't," Brannon said. "Nobody seems to know him on sight."

"Somebody must have brought him in and hired him just to kill me," Fargo said.

"Or maybe he just happened to recognize you and thought he'd make a name for himself."

"Right," Fargo said, "he just happened to be walking by the Judd house, looked in the window, saw me, and decided to take a shot at me."

"So then who do you think hired him?" Brannon said.

"I don't know, Sheriff," Fargo said. "That's your job."

"And what about your job?" Brannon asked. "Have you decided to work for Mr. Layton?"

"As a matter of fact, I have," Fargo said. "I guess that means we're working for the same man."

"Me? I, uh, don't work for Mr. Layton. I work for the town."

"Oh, yeah, that's right," Fargo said. "Excuse me for getting that wrong."

At that moment the door burst open and a man ran in, so breathless he couldn't talk right away.

"What the hell are ya doin', Harve?" Brannon shouted.

"Sheriff . . . ya gotta come . . . quick . . ."

"Why? What's goin' on?"

"Tad . . . Tad Layton . . ." the man said, breathlessly.

"Tad Layton? What about him? He got himself in trouble again?"

"Bad . . . it's bad . . . Sheriff . . ."

"Harve," Brannon said, "if you don't tell me what you're talkin' about—"

"Dead," Harve said finally. "Tad's . . . dead . . ."

Fargo went along with the sheriff, since technically speaking, he was working for the Layton family, now.

The man named Harve led them to the far south end of town, where Tad Layton was lying facedown in a ditch, the back of his head blown off.

"Oh, shit," Brannon said.

"Are you sure that's Tad Layton?" Fargo asked.

Harve and Sheriff Brannon looked at each other.

"Who found him, Harve?" Brannon asked.

"I did."

"Did you roll him over for a look?"

"Well, uh, no!"

"Then how do you know it's Tad Layton?"

"Well, it, uh, looks like Tad. Them's the clothes he was wearing last night, and that's Tad's gun."

74

"Better take a look, Sheriff," Fargo said. "You wouldn't want to tell Ben Layton one of his sons is dead, and then find out it's not him, would you?"

Brannon made a face, then looked at Harve.

"Roll him over, Harve."

"Why me?"

"Because you found him."

"But it's your job."

While the two men bickered Fargo stepped down into the ditch, took hold of one of the corpse's shoulders and rolled it over.

"Well?" he asked the two men.

Both of them looked at the body and then Brannon said, "That's Tad Layton."

"Henry Judd done it," Harve said.

Brannon and Fargo looked at him.

"Did you see him do it?" Fargo asked.

"Well, no . . ."

"Do you even know that Henry Judd was in town last night?"

"Uh, no . . ."

"Then why do you say he did it?"

" 'Cause everybody knows Tad was gonna take a prime piece of Henry's land."

"That's a motive," Sheriff Brannon agreed.

"But not proof, Sheriff," Fargo said, "and you need proof before you can go accusing a man of murder, let alone arrest him for it."

"Harve," Brannon said, "go get Doc Adams, and get some men to help you carry Tad into town once Doc's had a look at him."

"Why me—"

"Just do it!" Fargo snapped.

Harve shut up and hurried away.

"You got any deputies, Sheriff?"

"No," Brannon said, "when the town hired me they said they had no budget for deputies. Why, you wanna be one?"

"Not me," Fargo said. "Not with Ben Layton's son lying there dead. I wouldn't want to be wearing a badge in this town when he finds out. Oh, hey, you're going to have to tell him, aren't you?"

"Shit!" Brannon said again.

Doc Adams examined the body and then told Brannon he could have it moved.

"What killed him, Doc?" Brannon asked as the body was carried to the undertaker's.

"No secret about that," Adams said. "Somebody shot him in the face, and the bullet took out the back of his head. He was dead before he knew what hit him. Guess you're gonna have to tell old Ben about this."

"Andrea Layton was in town this morning," Fargo said.

"She was?" Brannon's look was hopeful. Maybe he could tell her, and she could tell her father.

"She was looking for her brothers," Fargo went on. "Found Lonnie in the saloon. Dave, the bartender, told her Andy was playing poker with somebody named Hutching."

"Will Hutching?" Brannon asked.

"That was the name."

"Did Dave say where Tad was?"

"No, he said he hadn't seen him. Even Lonnie said he hadn't seen Tad since earlier yesterday evening."

"Guess I better get over to Will's and see if they're

still there. I'd rather tell any of the three of them than have to tell Ben."

"Good luck," Adams said.

"You comin'?" Brannon asked Fargo.

"Not me," Fargo said. "I don't want any part of this."

"You came this far with me," Brannon said. He was obviously looking for somebody to back him up.

"Just out of curiosity, Sheriff. I'm done."

"Doc?"

"Not me, Sheriff," Doc Adams said. "This is your job."

Brannon scowled and then walked away from the ditch slowly.

"How are your legs?" Adams asked now that they were alone.

"Holding me up, so far."

"What do you think happened here?"

"I don't know," Fargo said. "Could have been anything, a robbery, a fight over a woman, or money."

"How do you stand with the Laytons right now?"

"I guess I work for Ben," Fargo said. "I talked with Andrea this morning, told her I was taking the job her father sent for me to do."

"Which is?"

"I don't know, yet."

"Well," Adams said, "I'm thinkin' maybe the job's gonna change now."

"Why?"

"He'll probably want you to find out who killed Tad."

"I'm no detective," Fargo said. "That's Brannon's job."

"Him?" Doc Adams didn't say anything else, but his tone said it all.

Fargo decided to take a seat in front of his hotel and see how the situation developed.

Sheriff Brannon had apparently found the rest of the Layton family at Will Hutching's poker game because they all came trooping down the street to the undertaker's office, which was visible from Fargo's vantage point. He recognized Lonnie Layton, and brother Andy was just an older, more mature version. However, it was Andrea who was in the lead, with her brothers trying to catch up. Sheriff Brannon was bringing up the rear, and didn't look happy.

After a few moments Andrea and Andy came out, looked around and spotted Fargo in front of the hotel. They crossed the street and mounted the boardwalk.

"Fargo, this is my brother, Andy," Andrea said.

"You heard about my brother Tad?" Andy asked, without preamble.

"I have. I'm sorry—"

"I don't want you to be sorry," Andy said, "I want you to find out who killed my brother."

"I'm not a detective, Mr. Layton," Fargo said. "Finding your brother's killer is the sheriff's job."

"Him! He's useless. Look, my father will pay you a lot of money to find Tad's killer."

"He was going to pay me a lot of money, anyway," Fargo said, "to do another job."

"Fargo," Andrea said, "please, you have to do this for us."

Fargo addressed himself to Andrea.

"What if your father doesn't want me involved in this?" he asked.

"All right, then," Andy said, "come out to the house with us today and we'll talk to him."

"I think I should come out tomorrow."

"Why tomorrow?" Andy asked.

"Because today you have to go out and break the news to your father. I think the family needs to be alone tonight, to figure out what you're going to do. I'll come out to the house in the morning." He looked at Andrea. "I promise."

Andrea put her hand on her brother's arm.

"He's right, Andy. Come on, we'll want to take Tad's body back with us. We have to get a buckboard."

"You're gonna find the man who killed my brother, Fargo," Andy said, "and then I'm gonna kill him."

"Come on, Andy."

Andrea tossed Fargo a look as she pushed her brother off the boardwalk into the street. Fargo found it odd that her eyes were completely dry. Andy seemed to be the most upset, although he wasn't shedding any tears, either. Fargo wondered how Ben Layton was going to take the news of his son's death.

Fargo remained in front of the hotel and watched as the undertaker loaded Tad Layton's remains onto a buckboard to be driven out to the Layton ranch. Fargo was sure a family that wealthy had their own cemetery, possibly where Andrea and the boys' mother was buried.

Watching the family climb aboard the buckboard after tying their horses to the back, Fargo suddenly realized something. Andrea had to be older than she looked, because she and Andy—Andrea and Andy—were obviously twins. That made her closer to thirty than twenty, and she looked damned good.

So she and her brother Andy were the oldest, with Tad and Lonnie next—only Tad was gone now.

Fargo found this to be quite a coincidence, that Tad should be killed just as he came to town. What if Henry Judd was the killer? After all, Tad *was* going to take some of his land, and maybe Henry was just sick and tired of having things taken from him. Once Fargo found out that it wasn't Henry who had sent for him Henry's chance of having Fargo help him was gone. Maybe he decided to take matters into his own hands.

And what if it was one of the Layton boys who bushwhacked Fargo and took his horse? Wouldn't that give Fargo a motive to kill one of them? Perhaps the killer—Henry Judd, or whoever—was hoping suspicion would fall on Fargo.

He saw the sheriff come out of the undertaker's office and come across the street toward him.

"I'm glad that's over with," Brannon said, mounting the boardwalk.

"Is it? Or is it just starting?"

"The family wants you to find the killer," Brannon said. "Andy said that's what his father will want, and they'll pay you a lot of money to do it. That means I'm out of it."

"I told you, and I told them, and I'll tell Ben Layton, I'm not a detective. If he wants to send for someone, that's his business."

"No chance," Brannon said. "They're too impressed with your reputation. I don't know what the original reason was that Ben sent for you, but that's gonna be forgotten now. Finding Tad's killer is going to be more important to them."

"Sheriff, I've been told that Lonnie likes horses." Brannon frowned.

"Yeah, Lonnie's got a bunch of horses. So what?"

"Where does he keep them?"

"Somewhere on the Layton property."

"Not in a corral near the house?"

"Lonnie keeps his horses away from the house. Say, are you thinking that maybe Lonnie stole your horse?"

Fargo was thinking that maybe Brannon wasn't as dumb as he looked, but he didn't say anything.

"Why would he do that, if it was his father who sent for you?"

"I don't know, Sheriff. Why would he?"

"He wouldn't," Brannon said. "Lonnie would no more cross his old man than . . ."

"Than you would?"

"Ben Layton gets what he wants in this valley, Fargo," Sheriff Brannon said. "You'd do well to remember that."

Brannon turned and walked away from the hotel, leaving Fargo to ponder his last words.

9

The next morning when Fargo woke up his legs worked fine and his back ached less. He went to the livery, saddled the horse he still had to bring back to Henry Judd and rode out to the Layton ranch. Since he was working for Ben Layton now he could probably get an even better horse from him. That would give him an excuse to go back to the Judd place to talk to Henry about the killing of Tad Layton.

When he reached the Layton house they were ready for him.

"I'll take the horse, Mr. Fargo," a hand said, and he handed the reins over to the man, whom he had never seen before. Apparently, everyone had been alerted that he was coming, and they were going to cooperate with him.

Another hand came over and said, "I'll take you into the house."

"That's fine," Fargo said.

The man led Fargo up the stairs to the front door but before they reached it, it opened and Andrea Layton stepped out.

"True to your word, I see," she said.

"Always."

He was surprised at her appearance. She was wearing a high-necked dress, dark blue, that covered her body quite well, except for the thrust of her peach breasts.

She noticed him looking at her and said, "I don't have a black dress. This is the closest I could come to something for mourning. Come on, I'll take you to my father. I've got him, Jake," she said to the hand.

"Yes, Miss Andrea. Uh, ma'am?"

"Yes?"

"Me and the boys, well, we're real sorry about Tad."

"Thank you, Jake," she said, "and thank the men, too."

"Yes, ma'am, I will."

"Fargo?"

He followed her into the house, waited while she closed the door.

"You and Andy are twins," he said as she turned to face him.

"Yes. Come this way."

He tracked her to the library, where Ben Layton was waiting this time.

"Fargo," Layton said, "glad you could come. Brandy?"

"Thank you, yes."

"Andrea?"

She nodded and went to get the brandy.

Layton was sitting in the same armchair he'd occupied the last time Fargo was there. He was wearing a dark suit, a boiled white shirt, and shiny boots.

"We're waiting for the priest to come from town," he said. "We're going to bury my boy today, next to his mother."

"I'm sorry about your son, Mr. Layton." Fargo accepted the brandy from Andrea. She then went to the sofa and sat, her hands demurely in her lap.

"Fargo, I sent for you because somebody was stealing cattle from me," Layton said. "You're concerned that you can't remember that, but the truth of the matter is we never did discuss why I wanted you, just what I was going to pay you."

"Thank you for that," Fargo said, his memory jogged. "I recall that now."

"But now something else has come up, as you well know. My boy has been killed, and the sheriff is in no way equipped to find out who. I want you to do it."

"Mr. Layton, I'm not—"

"I've heard your objections, I know what you said to Andy and Andrea. It doesn't matter. You'll still do a better job of it than the sheriff. He's too afraid of me."

"And I'm not?"

"On no, Mr. Fargo," Layton said, "you're not afraid of me, at all. You don't care that I might very well be the first governor of this territory. That's why I like you. Whatever you find out, you'll tell me. You won't whitewash it. If you discover that my son was killed while trying to rob someone, you'll tell me."

"Father!"

"I'm just making a point, my dear," Layton said. "I don't for a moment think that was the case."

"You are right, though," Fargo said. "If I was to do this I would tell you everything I find out, good or bad."

"That's what I want."

"And you'd have to tell me everything."

"Like what?"

84

"Like what Tad was up to. What all your boys are into."

"Why all of them?"

"Tad may have been killed because he was in the wrong place at the wrong time. Maybe he was killed by someone with a grudge against Andy, or Lonnie, but Tad was the Layton who was there."

"If that was the case," Layton said, "then he might have been killed to get to me."

"That's another possibility, yes."

"You see?" Layton said. "Already you've thought of something I didn't, something our sheriff never would have thought of. I'll pay you very well, Mr. Fargo, very well, indeed. Will you do this for me? For my family?"

"Mr. Layton," Fargo said, "you're aware I was shot, and my horse stolen."

"Yes, I am."

"Finding the man who did that to me is my first priority. I want you to know that. I don't take kindly to having someone try to kill me."

"I can understand that."

"Sir, if I find out it was one of your sons, I'll take action. Do you understand *that*?"

"I do."

"And knowing that you still want to hire me?"

"I do."

Fargo finished the brandy and put the glass down.

"All right, then, I'll do it."

"How much do you want?"

"We agreed on an amount, as I now recall," Fargo said. "That sum will do fine."

"Andrea," Layton said, "go to my office and bring the cash that's in the safe."

"How much of it, Father?"

"All of it."

Her eyes widened.

"All of it?"

"Yes," he said.

"But, Pa—"

"Do it, girl."

"Yes, Father."

As she left the room Fargo said, "You rely on her heavily don't you?"

"I do," Layton said, "and I have, ever since her mother died. It's not fair to her, I know. I wish she would marry and leave this place."

"Have you told her that?"

"Yes, but she won't listen. Besides, she says there are no men around here fit to marry, and since she won't leave here she's resigned herself to being an old maid."

"Why won't she leave?"

"Because it's a new territory, and if I'm to become governor she thinks—she *knows*—I'll need her help. Fargo, this territory won't always be miners and speculators and gamblers out to take their money. The mines will dry up eventually, and someone will have to be in a position to keep the territory from drying up, as well."

"And that would be you, Mr. Layton?"

"A lot of people think so," Ben Layton said, "people from Washington. People who know about these things."

Fargo was suddenly aware of the fact that Ben Layton was somewhat insecure about himself. Sure, others felt he'd be a good governor, but Layton himself seemed to have his doubts.

"But we're not here to talk about me being governor," Layton said. "I can't even think about that, in fact, until we find out who killed Tad."

"If I'm going to do that I'd like to be able to talk to your other two sons."

"I'll make sure they talk to you."

"And your hands."

"Why them?"

"One of them, or some of them, might know something about Tad that you, or his brothers, don't."

"That's ridiculous," Layton said. "How would they know more about him than his family?"

"Are you that close a family?"

"Of course we are," Layton said. "By the very definition a *family* is close, don't you think?"

"I don't know," Fargo said. "I've never been part of one."

"Then you're missing out. You're still a young man, you have time to get married, have kids—"

"If we could get back to the subject," Fargo said. He didn't know if Layton was singing the praises of marriage and a family because he had an eligible daughter.

"Of course," Layton said. "You'll have everything you need."

"I'll need the sheriff to talk to me truthfully."

"He will."

"He is, I take it, for want of a better phrase, in your pocket."

Layton straightened his back and said, "He's my

man, if that's what you mean. I picked him, and put him in office."

"Why, if I may ask?"

"Why what?"

"Why him? Why not a man who was more competent?"

Layton seemed to consider the wisdom of answering that question honestly, and then went ahead and did so.

"A more competent man—such as yourself, for example—would not be so easy to control."

Fargo was surprised by the man's candor. He'd expected a different kind of answer.

Before he could ask another question Andrea reappeared carrying an envelope.

"Just hand it to Mr. Fargo, my dear," her father said.

"But, Father, don't you want to count it?"

"I know how much is there, Andrea. Just give it to Mr. Fargo like a good girl."

Andrea hesitated, then walked to Fargo and handed him the envelope, which was thick with cash. Fargo could see that she was upset about something, but she didn't question her father in front of him. He wondered if she'd even question him later.

"Thank you."

"Andrea, would you let the hands know that they're to answer all of Mr. Fargo's questions?"

"Yes, Father."

"I'll talk to your brothers about the same thing."

"All right."

"Mr. Fargo? I'd like to offer you the hospitality of my home while you're working for me. We have rooms upstairs—"

"No offense meant, Mr. Layton, but I'd just as soon stay at the hotel in town. That's where the killing took place, after all."

"No offense taken, sir," Layton said. "I see your point."

Fargo stood up and Layton did the same.

"I'd best get started. Oh, I will need one more thing before I go."

"What's that?"

"A horse," Fargo said, "a good one. The one I have has to be returned to Henry Judd."

"You'll have your choice of my stock," Layton said. "My foreman's name is Dack Sessions. Andrea will introduce you. He'll see to it that you get a fine horse."

"Thank you."

"And it's yours, even when you're finished working for me," Layton said. "Consider it a bonus."

"Again," Fargo said, "no offense meant, but by the time I leave here I expect to have my own horse back."

"Oh, yes," Layton said, "I'd forgotten your intent to reclaim your own horse. What makes you think the animal is still in this valley?"

"I don't know that it is," Fargo said, "but rest assured if it is, I'll find it."

"You have a great deal of love for a horse."

"Not at all," Fargo said. "Love has nothing to do with it, but that Ovaro is mine and somebody took it from me."

There was an awkward moment when Fargo's intentions hung naked in the air, and then Layton said, "Again, I see your point. Andrea, would you introduce Mr. Fargo to Dack?"

"Yes, Father," she said, and led Fargo from the room, and the house.

"I hate when he gets like that," Andrea complained outside.

"Like what?"

"Like I'm his little girl and I'm here to run his errands."

"How does he usually treat you?"

"Half the time like that."

"And the other half?"

"Like he couldn't make a decision without me."

"If it's any consolation he seems to think he couldn't become governor without you."

"Nice try," she said, "but I happen to know that he wishes I'd get married. *I'm* the one who doesn't think he can be governor without me."

Fargo didn't comment on that.

"Where the hell is—oh, there he is. Dack!"

The foreman, Dack Sessions, turned out to be a man in his midthirties, tall and rangy with a slanted jaw and—when he took off his hat—a widow's peak. Fargo could also tell something else just by looking at the man—he was in love with Andrea Layton. It was written all over his face.

"Dack, this is Skye Fargo. He's working for my—for us now, and he needs a horse—a good one."

"All we've got is good ones, Miss Andrea," Sessions said.

"Would you see to it that he gets one?"

"I sure will—and, Andrea, I'm real sorry about Tad."

"I know, Dack. That's what Mr. Fargo is here about. We want him to find out who killed Tad."

"I see."

"Would you tell the men they're to talk to him and tell him anything he wants to know?"

"I'll tell 'em."

"Good." She turned to Fargo. "Come and see me before you leave."

"All right."

She touched the foreman on the arm and said, "Thanks, Dack."

"My pleasure, Miss Andrea," Sessions said. As she walked away the man turned to Fargo. "I know your rep, Mr. Fargo. I don't guess you'll need any help picking out a horse."

"No," Fargo said. "Just show me the stock and I'll do the rest."

"That's fine, then," Sessions said. "Just come this way."

10

Fargo didn't expect to find the Ovaro in among the Layton stock, and he didn't. What he did find was a gelding that suited him, one that was about four and stood about seventeen hands.

"He's a big one, all right," Sessions said, "but that gray over there's a better animal, and that roan is built for speed—"

"I don't need speed," Fargo said, examining the gelding's legs. "I'm not going to race anybody."

"Well, suit yourself. If you want that gelding I guess he's yours. Do you need a saddle?"

"Yes." He decided to return the saddle he'd borrowed from the Judds, also.

"I'll see what I can find for you."

"I appreciate it."

While the foreman was hunting up a saddle Fargo took the gelding from the corral into the barn. When Sessions returned he didn't look happy, but he was carrying a beautiful black silver-embossed saddle.

"Mr. Layton says you're to have his saddle."

"Tell Mr. Layton I appreciate the offer but this kind of saddle would make me a moving target during the day, with the sun reflecting off all that silver. I saw a worn saddle in the back of the barn earlier. I'll just take that one."

Sessions carefully laid aside his boss's saddle and once again said, "Suit yourself."

He went to the back of the barn and brought back a worn but usable saddle. Fargo accepted it and set about to saddling the gelding.

Sessions picked up the silver-embossed saddle as if to leave, and Fargo stopped him.

"Before I talk to the men I'd like to talk to you."

"About what?" Sessions set the saddle down.

"Tad Layton."

"What about him? He's dead."

"Somebody killed him, and didn't rob him." He'd learned that much from the sheriff. Layton's pockets had not been cleaned, and he still had plenty of money on him.

"So?"

"Why would someone want to kill him?"

"How would I know."

"You're the foreman. You worked with him, didn't you?"

Sessions snorted.

"What makes you think he did any work around here?" the foreman asked.

"He didn't?"

"Hell, no."

"Did any of the other boys?"

"Andy's the only one who works," Sessions said, "and that's because he knows this ranch will be his, soon."

"Soon? Is he expecting his father to die?"

"No, to become governor. When that happens he'll

probably go and live in Silver City, or someplace like that. That will make the ranch Andy's."

"So Lonnie doesn't do any work, either?"

Again the derisive snort.

"Even less than Tad, if that's possible."

"I understood Lonnie had a way with horses. He doesn't work the stock?"

"He works his own stock."

"And where does he keep them?"

"In a canyon north of here. It's sort of a natural corral. He goes out there every day and works the horses."

"Is he good at it?"

"From what I can see, yeah."

"Then why doesn't his old man make him work with you?"

" 'Cause he lets those boys do whatever they damn well please, that's why."

"And what about Andrea?"

The foreman's face immediately softened.

"Andrea's different. She doesn't have to work the ranch. She helps her father with the paperwork, but she comes out and works with us every once in a while, anyway."

"He seems to rely pretty heavily on her."

"Not as much as he should, in my opinion," Sessions said. "She's real smart, and he's not using her enough."

Fargo tightened the cinch on the saddle and saw that it had been repaired recently. He thought it would hold, for a while.

He turned to face Sessions.

"What was Tad into, Mr. Sessions?"

"Don't call me mister," the foreman said. "Just Dack, or Sessions, if you want."

"What was he into, Dack?"

"What do you mean?"

"What got him killed?"

"I told you," Sessions said. "I didn't know him that well."

"Do you know Andy?"

"Andy and I go back a ways," Sessions said. In that moment Fargo realized that he had overestimated the man's age. He was probably more Andy's age, but he looked older because he looked weathered. Also, the widow's peak didn't help.

"Would anyone have killed Tad to get to Andy?"

"Not anybody that knew him."

"Why not?"

"Because Andy hated Tad."

"He hated his brother?"

"Like the plague."

"And Lonnie?"

Sessions shook his head.

"He had no use for Lonnie, either."

"What about Andrea?"

"They're twins," the foreman said, as if that explained it all.

"And what about his father?"

"All three of them boys go their own way, but they all love—loved—that old man."

Fargo frowned. Was Ben Layton really laboring under the impression that his family was a close one? Or had he simply been lying?

He decided to put the question to the foreman, who frowned and scowled when asked.

"Mr. Layton believes whatever he wants to believe," he said. "I don't question him. You see, I love that old man, too."

"What kind of a governor do you think he'll make?"

"A great one."

"Do you think somebody might have killed Tad to get to him?"

"Now that's a possibility."

"Okay, Dack," Fargo said, "thanks for your help. I'll be around for a while, talking to the men."

"That's fine, but you won't get much out of them. Tad didn't associate with them much, either."

"Who did he run with?"

"Lonnie, mostly," Sessions said, "when he did run with somebody, but for the most part they all went their own way."

"I better talk to Lonnie, then," Fargo said, wondering if Lonnie was the one who had shot him and stolen his horse. He was going to have to find this canyon of Lonnie's and take a look at his stock. If he stole the Ovaro, he was probably keeping it there.

"I have to return the boss's saddle and get to work," Sessions said.

"Okay, fine. I'll tell Mr. Layton you were real helpful."

Sessions nodded, picked up the saddle, and left the barn.

Fargo left the gelding in the barn and went to find one of the Layton boys. The one he came across was Andy, and found him by following the sound of shooting out in back of the house. When he reached there he saw that Andy Layton was practicing shooting his pistol, having set up a huge collection of bottles and cans along a fence. As Fargo approached Andy was ejecting the spent shells from his gun and loading in live ones, six of them. He holstered his gun and turned at the sound of Fargo's footsteps.

"What are you practicing for?" Fargo asked. "Are you expecting a war?"

"Maybe a small one," Andy said. He drew and fired and a can jumped off the fence.

"Impressive."

Andy looked over his shoulder at Fargo.

"Aren't you supposed to be looking for who killed my brother? Or is there something you want to ask me?"

"Both," Fargo said. "I was wondering if you might have an idea who'd want to kill your brother."

"Specifically," Andy said, "I wouldn't know. Tad pretty much went his own way. He liked throwing Pa's weight around, though."

"Not his own?"

Andy snorted.

"Tad didn't have any weight to throw," he said. "No, he just slung the old man's around, hit people in the face with it, over the head with it. He had a habit of takin' what he wanted. I guess maybe he finally tried it with the wrong person."

"But you wouldn't have any idea who that might be?"

"Nope."

"What about Henry Judd."

"He wouldn't have the nerve."

"Could he have been killed by mistake?"

"Instead of who?"

97

"You? Lonnie? Maybe your father?"

"My father hardly goes into town, anymore," Andy said. "I don't look much like Tad, and you'll have to ask Lonnie if he's gotten anybody mad at him, lately, but he don't look much like Tad, either. No, my guess is whoever killed him knew they were killin' Tad." He snapped off another shot, shattering a bottle. "That's my guess, for whatever it's worth."

"Andy, your father thinks that you, and your brothers, and Andrea, and he are one big happy family."

Fargo had caught Andy as he was about to snap off another shot. He jerked the trigger and missed his intended target. He turned and looked directly at Fargo for the first time.

"You want me to talk about my family?"

"If you will."

Andy studied him a few more moments, then looked away, at the array of bottles and cans on the fence.

"See that smaller can, at the far right?"

"I see it."

"I was saving it for last," Andy said. "Do you know why?"

"No, why?"

"Because I'm not sure I can hit it from here," Andy admitted. "All of this shooting is building up to eventually taking a shot at that can. That can has been there for months. Today was the day I thought I'd hit it."

"So?"

"If you hit that can I'll tell you everything you want to know about my family."

"I'm not a gunfighter," Fargo said.

"I know your reputation, Fargo," Andy said. "You're a man who gets things done."

"That's how I think of myself."

"Okay, then," Andy said, "you want me to talk to you about my family, and the way to get that done is to hit that can."

"And if I don't?"

"Then I'll still be trying, probably for months," Andy said, "and I won't be feeling very talkative."

Fargo looked at the can, which seemed very small, indeed.

"I want to see that can fl—" Andy started, but Fargo drew his gun and fired at the can. It wasn't a snap draw, but a very deliberate one, and the can went flying in the air.

"What do you want to know?" Andy Layton asked.

Andy explained that the only family member he felt close to was Andrea, because they were twins. He didn't get along with his brothers, but he didn't want them dead. As for his father, he loved him, but he wished he'd be appointed governor already and move away so Andy could have the ranch.

"Okay," Fargo said, "that explains your relationship with your family. What about their relationships with each other?"

"See that bottle, on the left?"

Fargo drew and shattered the bottle.

"The old man would be lost without Andrea," Andy said. "He could live without any of his three sons— well, two sons, now."

"All I ever heard was about the Layton boys, and how Ben Layton was proud of them."

"What's he got to be proud of?" Andy asked.

"You were real upset yesterday about your brother being killed."

"Hey," Andy said, "he was my brother. We didn't get along, but that don't mean somebody can kill him and I won't be doing anything about it."

"So family's family."

"That's right."

Fargo had an idea that Andy got this thinking from his father, Ben. Maybe they didn't get along, but they thought alike.

"Andy, I'm going to ask you another question, and I'll shoot as many bottles and cans as it takes to get the answer."

"Go ahead," Andy said, "ask."

"Do you think Lonnie might have shot me and stole my horse?"

"It's possible," Andy said, surprising Fargo with his candor. "He's a bad shot, and that would explain why you're still alive."

"Would he have put my horse in with his stock?"

"Maybe," Andy said. "He's dumb enough."

"Do you know where this canyon is where he keeps his horses?"

"I do."

"Would you take me there?"

Andy pointed at the fence.

"There ain't enough bottles and cans up there to make me take you there."

"Why not?"

"Because he's my brother," Andy said, "and you're not."

"Family's family, huh?"

100

"That's right." Andy ejected the spent shells from his gun and replaced them with live ones, then holstered the weapon. "I got work to do."

"Okay, thanks for talking to me."

"Thanks for taking care of that can for me," Andy said. "It's been botherin' me for months."

"Why not just walk up to it and knock it off the fence?"

"You know," Andy said with a shrug, "I just never thought of it."

As Andy turned away, Fargo drew his gun and shattered three more bottles in succession. Andy turned quickly to find Fargo ejecting spent shells from his Colt.

"Had to reload, anyway," Fargo said.

11

Fargo took his new horse out for a ride. He headed north with half an idea of finding Lonnie Layton's natural corral. The other half was just to get to know the horse a bit. The animal responded well to commands, but Fargo did miss the familiar feel of the Ovaro beneath him.

He had dismounted, giving his back a rest, when he heard a rider approaching. He turned and saw Andrea Layton riding toward him on a small, but athletic-looking pinto.

"Just out for a ride?" he asked when she reined in.

"No," she said, "I was looking for you."

"Why?"

"I had a talk with Andy."

"And?"

"He said you were looking for Lonnie's stock."

"That's right."

"I'll take you to them," she said. "I know where they are."

"Why would you do that?"

She leaned forward in her saddle.

"Because if Lonnie took your horse I want you to have it back."

"Why?"

"Because you won't give finding Tad's killer all your attention until you do."

"That's a good enough reason, I guess," Fargo said.

"Then get mounted. We've got to ride west a little ways, and then north again. You never would have found it on your own."

Andrea was right. Not only was the canyon a natural corral, with only one way in, but it was practically hidden from view, unless you knew where to look.

"It looks like a solid rock face but there's a sliver of an opening," Andrea explained, and he saw how right she was when she took him through it. If he had stuck both arms out from his sides he would have touched the wall on either side—but then he had long arms.

When they rode through the slim opening the canyon opened up and he saw the corral and gate that had been built right up against the walls. Only one length of corral fence was needed, and the rock face formed the other three sides. The horses couldn't get out, and if they did they'd only be able to file out of the canyon one at a time.

"It's ingenious," Fargo said.

"Yes," Andrea said, "and Lonnie lucked into it. Ingenious is a little beyond him."

Fargo rode back and forth in front of the fence, looking over the stock. Lonnie had about twenty horses there, all good-looking, wild specimens.

"Is yours there?"

"No."

"Are you sure?"

"He's an Ovaro," Fargo said, "with very distinctive markings. He's not there."

"Then I guess it wasn't Lonnie."

"Maybe not."

"Unless he put it somewhere else."

"Like where?"

"I don't know," she said. "This is the only place I know of."

"Well, thanks for bringing me here."

"I wish the horse was here," she said, "then you'd have him back and be able to concentrate on Tad's killer."

He didn't mention that first he would have had to have it out with Lonnie, who probably would have ended up dead. Then how would he have looked for the killer of one of her brothers when he was the killer of another?

Just as well the Ovaro wasn't there.

"I should get back to town," he said.

"I'll ride part of the way with you."

When Fargo got back to town his lower back was killing him. He had stopped at the Layton place to pick up the horse he'd borrowed from Henry Judd. When he got to town he left both the borrowed horse and his new gelding at the livery. During the walk back to the hotel his left leg started to go numb. He tried not to show it as he walked through the lobby and painfully up the stairs. When he got to his room he collapsed on the bed, and hoped he just needed a little rest to remedy the situation. What he didn't need right now was to show any weakness in public.

By now the word must have spread that he was working for the Laytons, looking for whoever had killed Tad. If the killer—whoever it was—thought he had a weakness he would look to exploit it.

He got his boots off and spent some time massaging the numb leg. Then he reclined on the bed and fell asleep. He woke several hours later and his legs felt fine. His back still ached some, but he could live with that.

He was thinking about getting something to eat and decided to wash up first. He stripped off his shirt, poured some water from a pitcher into a basin, and washed his face and his torso. He was drying himself with a towel when there was a knock at the door. He went to the bedpost first for his gun, draped the towel over it, put on some clothes and then answered the door.

It was Andrea Layton.

"What's under the towel?" she asked, walking past him into the room.

He closed the door, then removed the towel from the gun.

"You won't be needing that . . . unless you're afraid of me."

He walked to the bedpost and holstered the gun. When he turned she was right behind him and he almost bumped into her. She studied his bare chest, then put her hands on him, rubbing her palms over him.

"You're very strong," she said. "I like strong men."

"Andrea—"

"I told you before we were going to sleep together," she said. "We both knew it right away."

"With the way things were going . . ."

"You thought I changed my mind?" she asked. She licked her lips. "I want you more now than ever, Skye."

She lifted her head to be kissed and he obliged her. He slid his arms around her and gathered her to him. Her breasts were firm against his chest, and her tongue blossomed sweetly in his mouth.

She was dressed as she usually was, in a shirt and trousers. He pulled the shirt from her waistband and slid his hands beneath it. Her bare skin was soft, her breasts firm, the nipples like little pebbles against his palms. She moaned into his mouth as he pinched them, then pulled her mouth from his so she could gasp.

"Oooh, yes, Skye," she said, "I've been thinking about this. I want to be taken. Take off my clothes and take me to bed, Skye, please?"

He didn't need to be asked again. He undressed her hurriedly, tearing some buttons from the shirt as he did. He yanked off her boots and then pulled off her trousers and tossed them into a corner. There was only a wisp of cloth between them now and he tore that from her and pushed her down on the bed.

On her back she stretched as he removed the rest of his own clothes. Her belly was flat, her legs long and lean. The hair between her legs was a wiry tangle and he could smell the scent of her readiness wafting up from it.

He got on the bed with her and began to kiss and lick her nipples, then sucked them into his mouth to bite them. She caught her breath sharply, then let it out as his lips traveled down over her belly. Finally, his tongue probed into that tangle of hair while he kept his hands busy on her breasts.

"Oh, Skye, yes, oh yes, oh, oh, what are you . . . doing to me . . . oh, your tongue . . ."

His tongue probed deeper, tasting the sweet, wet, sticky depths of her, then withdrawing from her to find her hard little nub. He brought his hands down then, so he could cup her hard buttocks and lift her up so he could have complete access to her. He licked her moist slit up and down as she moaned, and cried out, and thrashed beneath him.

"Ooooh God, you're going to kill me . . . oh, yes, like that, yes, Skye, oh yes . . ." And then she just started saying that word over and over, with a long, sibilant sound at the end, "Yessss . . . yessss . . . yessss . . ."

And then she was bucking beneath him as her passions took hold of her, as her time came and she went over the edge, and he continued to lick her, suck her until she put her hands on his head to push him away because pleasure and pain were becoming one. . . .

He mounted her, then, not giving her time to recover. She wanted to be taken, and he was going to take her. He slid his hands beneath her, cupping her buttocks once again, driving himself into the wet, steamy depths of her. Her legs came up and wrapped around him and he began to move in and out of her, long, hard strokes that made her grunt every time he speared her again, and again, and again. . . .

She used her nails on his back, and her teeth on his shoulder as she came again, crying out, imploring him never to stop, and then he was there with her, exploding into her, and she seemed to be sucking him in, more and more, demanding more from him, pleading with him to make it go on forever and ever and never stop. She said it over and over again, "Never stop . . . never stop . . . never stop . . . nevernevernever . . ."

*   *   *

Afterward they lay together on the bed, his arm around her, her body pressed tightly to his. He marveled at how firm her body was, he couldn't have found an inch of extra flesh to pinch between his fingers.

"I knew it would be like that," she said. "I knew it. Even though it's never been that way with anyone else. I knew it would be with you."

"You're sweet, Andrea," he said, "and incredible."

She kissed his chest, then ran her palm over it again, enjoying the way the hard slabs felt beneath her skin.

"I think about leaving here, sometimes."

"I didn't think you did," he said. "Not after what your father said."

"By now you've talked to Andy," she said. "He's probably told you we're not quite the happy family my father would like to think we are."

"Then if you've thought about leaving, why don't you?"

"Because that's all it is," she said, "a thought, a dream, a . . . fantasy. I have to stay and help run the ranch, especially if Father is made governor."

"Andy can't run the ranch?"

"Not without me," she said. "He can't do anything without me, to tell you the truth."

"And Lonnie?"

"I'm the only one Lonnie ever talks to, and he doesn't even tell me everything."

"Would he be any help running the ranch?"

"He could, if he wanted to be," she said. "He's very good with horses. He could handle them, while Andy handled the cattle and I did the paperwork . . . if we were a family that worked together, we'd do very well."

"Well, it sounds like if anyone could pull them together, you could. What about Tad? How much help would he have been?"

"Not much," she said. "Tad was very selfish, and he kept to himself. He didn't really talk to any of us, except once in a while to Lonnie."

"Then maybe Lonnie knows why he was killed," Fargo said. "I'll have to talk to him tomorrow."

"And what about your search for your horse? Is that over?"

"No," he said, "although it's beginning to look like it might not have been your brother. Could it have been Tad, Andrea?"

"Why would he do it?"

"I don't know," Fargo said, "but you said he kept to himself, so who would have known what his motive was?"

"I don't want to talk about this anymore," she said. "In fact, I don't want to talk."

She rolled on top of him, straddling him, and began to rub her still-wet cleft up and down the length of his penis. She leaned over so he could kiss her breasts, holding them in his hands while he nibbled on them. She became wetter and wetter, while he swelled larger and larger, and then she lifted her hips, held him firmly, and impaled herself on him.

"Now," she said, huskily, "I'm going to take you . . ."

12

Andrea stayed all night and they made love the next morning.

"What's your father going to say about you being out all night?" Fargo asked as they dressed to go downstairs for breakfast.

"He won't know," she said. "He'll think I was home all night and left the house early this morning."

"He'll think that," Fargo asked, "or convince himself of that?"

"With my father it's the same thing."

"And what about the town?"

"What about it?"

"I mean the people," he said. "What are they going to say when we have breakfast together?"

"Who cares what they think," Andrea said, "and they won't say anything because they're afraid of my father."

"Afraid of him?"

"Afraid that, if he moves away, the town will die."

"How much of it does he own?"

"Probably half. See, they'll do anything to keep him from leaving. The town—hell, the territory—isn't old enough to survive without him."

"And what happens when he's made governor? He'll move away, then."

"But he'll be part of the larger picture," she said. "And the ranch will still be here."

They went downstairs and had breakfast in the hotel dining room.

"What are you going to do today?" she asked over coffee. All she had with it was some toast and jam, while Fargo had a full breakfast of eggs, and ham and biscuits.

"I've got to return a horse to Henry Judd, and then I want to talk to your brother, Lonnie."

"I'll try to make sure he's around so you can find him," she said. "Tell me, while you were a guest of the Judds, what did you think of Karen?"

"She's very lovely, and she took good care of me."

"I'll bet," Andrea said. "Did she tell you that she almost married my father?"

"Yes."

"Did she also tell you that she slept with Andy?"

"Yes."

"Well," Andrea said, surprised, "you two must have got on real well for her to tell you all of that."

"We talked a lot. Did, uh, your father know about Andy and Karen?"

"I'm not sure," she said. "That might be one of the things he pretends didn't happen."

"But he called off the wedding, right?"

"No," Andrea said bitterly, "she did. Almost broke his heart."

"And what about Andy?"

"What about him?"

111

"Why did he sleep with the woman his father was going to marry?"

"You saw Karen," Andrea said. "She wanted Andy, and she got him. He's not very strong-minded, you know. He couldn't have resisted her."

"You're saying she seduced him?"

"Well, of course. Andy's really not very interested in women, not the way Lonnie is. He never would have gone after her on his own."

"I see."

They finished breakfast and left the hotel together.

"I'm going back out to the ranch to make sure Lonnie stays put."

"I'll come by after I stop at the Judd place."

She put her hand on his arm and said, "I'll see you later, then."

She didn't care what the town thought or did, but that didn't mean she was going to kiss him out there in front of everyone.

Fargo saddled his new gelding, then the borrowed horse, and rode out to the Judd house. When he arrived he found Karen out in front of the house, sweeping off the porch. She leaned on the broom as he approached, no look of welcome on her face.

"What do you want?" she demanded.

"Why the hostility, Karen?" he asked. "I thought we were friends."

"You work for Ben Layton," she said. "That makes you no friend of mine."

"I admire your newfound devotion to your husband," he said wryly.

"My feelings about Ben have got nothing to do with Henry," she said, but did not elaborate.

"Is Henry around?"

"He's working."

"I brought back the horse and saddle he loaned me."

"Leave it right there," she said. "He'll put it away when he gets home."

"I don't understand your attitude, Karen," Fargo said. "I was the one who was being lied to while I was here."

"*I* never lied to you," she said. "I told you what I wanted and you gave it to me. Now I bet you're giving it to that bitch, Andrea."

Fargo didn't reply and didn't let anything show on his face. If Karen expected to find an answer there she would be disappointed.

"Henry lied about sending for me," Fargo said. "He knew all along that it was Ben Layton I was here to work for."

"So?"

"So he used my injuries to mislead me. I hate dishonesty, Karen, in a man or a woman."

"Like I said before," she replied, "I was never dishonest. If Henry was, you'll have to take it up with him."

"Where is he?"

"Mending a fence."

"Where?"

She glared at him, then gave him directions.

"Much obliged, Karen."

"Don't thank me, Fargo."

He rode away from the house in the direction she'd given him, realizing that, once again, she was being truthful to him. She had been very open and truthful while he'd been a "guest," and now again she was telling the truth. She didn't want to have anything to do with him while he was working for Ben Layton. Whatever had happened between her and the elder Layton, Fargo felt it had more to do with just her sleeping with Andy.

Much more.

Fargo found Henry Judd where Karen said he would, but he'd expected to find a couple of hands working with him. Instead, Henry was alone.

He stopped working on a fencepost he was securing and watched as Fargo approached.

"What do you want?" he asked, giving Fargo the same welcome Karen had.

"I brought back the horse you loaned me."

"Shoulda rented it to you," Henry said. "I showed you the hospitality of my home and you betrayed me."

"Henry," Fargo said, "it wasn't my intention to sleep with your wife, believe me."

"I'm not talking about that," Henry said. "I'm talking about you working for Ben Layton."

"He's the one who sent for me, remember?" Fargo asked. "Or have you started believing your own lies?"

"I only lied because I needed help," Henry said.

"Where are your hands?"

"Gone."

"Why?"

"When they heard that Layton had hired the Trailsman they hightailed it. Now I've got to run this place all alone."

"You have Karen."

Henry snorted.

"She'll be the next to leave, you just watch. Then I'll really be alone."

"Henry, you were the first one to insinuate that Lonnie Layton shot me and stole my horse."

"So?"

"So I've seen where he keeps his horses and mine isn't there."

"That doesn't mean he didn't steal it."

"No, it doesn't, but it does make it unlikely."

"So are you here to accuse me?"

"No, I'm here to ask you if you know anything for sure about it."

"All I know is that we found you and nursed you back to health."

"You found me and gave me a room," Fargo said, "but the doctor treated me, and my health came back on its own."

"That's fine, then," Henry said. "Don't give us any credit."

"Henry, why don't you sell this place to Ben Layton?" Fargo asked.

"Never," Henry said stubbornly. "This is my place, I worked hard to get it and I worked hard to maintain it. I'm not selling."

"But if Karen leaves—"

"I didn't build it for her," he said, "I built it for me. I wanted a place of my own for years and I finally have it."

Fargo could sympathize with Henry Judd. While he'd never wanted a place of his own, he knew many people who had, and when they got it, it was like a dream come true. Henry Judd had his, and somebody—Ben Layton—was trying to take it away from him.

And then there was Tad, who had been about to take the choicest piece of land from him.

"Henry, do you know anything about Tad Layton's death?" Fargo asked.

"I know I'd like to pin a medal on whoever killed him," Henry said.

"It sure came at a convenient time for you."

"The sheriff already tried that line, Fargo," Henry said, "and it didn't work for him. He couldn't prove a thing, and do you know why?"

"Because he's not equipped to be a detective?"

"Because I didn't kill Tad, that's why."

"If you didn't, Henry," Fargo asked, "who did?"

"How would I know?"

"Where you in town that night?"

Henry hesitated, then said, "Yes. Why lie about it? Somebody is sure to have seen me. Yes, I was in town that night."

"Did you see Tad?"

Again he hesitated, and again he said, "Yes."

"You're going to make it very hard for me to suspect you, Henry, if you keep telling the truth like that."

"What else do you want to know?"

"Why did you go to see Tad?"

"I didn't go to see him," Henry said, "I ran into him on the street. He was falling-down drunk, so I helped him fall down."

"You pushed him?"

"I hit him," Henry said. "We had an argument about the piece of land he wanted. I tried to reason with him,

116

I even offered him other pieces, but he wouldn't back down, so I hit him."

"And then what happened?"

"He fell down and I left."

"Henry, how do you know you didn't kill him with that blow?"

"I don't have iron in my fists, Fargo," Henry said. "I'm not a fighter. I wouldn't even have hit him if he wasn't so drunk."

"So you never saw him after you hit him and left him on the ground?"

"No."

"Well," Fargo said, "if you didn't kill him, then somebody else came along and did."

"And God bless him."

"I wouldn't say that, Henry."

"Why not? The son of a bitch is dead and he's not gonna be takin' my land from me."

"Whoever killed him," Fargo said, "probably saw you hit him. They went over and finished him, and figured you'd take the blame."

"And how were they gonna blame me?"

"Probably by telling the sheriff they saw you with Tad."

"So whoever tells him that is the killer?"

"Could be," Fargo said. "I'd be surprised if it was that easy, but that just could be it."

13

Fargo went back to town to consider his options. His primary concern was still getting the Ovaro back and finding out who shot him and took it. If it turned out to be Tad he was going to feel cheated, but somehow he didn't think that was the case.

He had the feeling that by working for Layton and finding out who killed his son, he'd find his man, as well. He wasn't sure how he was going to do that, though. He wasn't a detective, but if he couldn't investigate he probably could ask questions as well as the next man.

So he walked around town, asking questions. Was anyone with Tad Layton that night? Did anyone see Tad Layton? Did anyone see Tad Layton with anyone else?

When he got tired of asking strangers questions, and having them look at him oddly, wondering who he was, why he was asking questions, and why they should answer him, he stopped into a café to get some early dinner. The man he still had to talk to was Lonnie Layton, the younger brother. To do that he was probably going to have to go back out to the Layton ranch.

Sitting over his dinner, his lower back started to

ache, either from the walking, the riding, or both. He hoped that the numbness in his legs had come back for the last time. He could put up with a little backache, but every time his legs "disappeared" on him there was the fear that, this time, they might not come back.

After dinner he went back out on the street but he didn't ask any questions, this time. He walked to the sheriff's office and entered. Brannon was at his desk and looked up as Fargo approached it.

"Mind if I sit?" Fargo asked.

"What's on your mind?"

"Cooperation."

"What kind of—"

"An exchange of information," Fargo said, "about Tad Layton's death."

"What makes you think I know anything," Brannon asked, "and why should I believe that you know anything?"

"I don't know much, I admit," Fargo said, "but I'd think you'd want to do what you could to help your benefactor."

"My benefactor?"

"And your future governor."

"Oh," Brannon said, "you mean Mr. Layton."

"The one and only."

"Well," Brannon said, "he brought you in over me, but I guess I could do what I can to help."

"I'm sure he'd be very grateful."

"What do you want to know?"

"Who had it in for Tad Layton," Fargo asked, "or any of the Laytons?"

"They're a rich family, Fargo," Brannon said. "The

question should probably be, who *didn't* have it in for them."

"Okay," Fargo said, "who didn't?"

"I don't know."

"Well then, we're back to who did," Fargo said, "and let's try to be precise."

"That's easy. Henry Judd."

"Do you really think Henry would have the nerve to kill Tad?"

"Yes," Brannon said.

"Why?"

"Two reasons," Brannon said. "Ben wanted his ranch, and Tad wanted a specific piece of land."

"I know all that."

"Then you know Henry probably did it."

Fargo decided not to tell the sheriff what Henry Judd had told him. The fact that Henry had knocked Tad down while he was drunk didn't mean he killed him, but it would have been enough for the sheriff to arrest him, and for some reason Fargo just didn't think Henry had done it. Henry Judd didn't have enough passion in him to kill. If he did he might have tried to kill Fargo for sleeping with his wife, instead of tolerating it.

"Okay, Sheriff," Fargo said, "thanks for talking to me."

"Hey," Brannon said as Fargo headed for the door, "what about your part of the bargain?"

"My part?" Fargo asked, opening the door.

"Sharing what you know with me?"

"Oh, that," Fargo said. "I will, Sheriff, as soon as I find out something."

Fargo went out the door before the sheriff could protest.

Fargo's next task was to find Lonnie and question him. He rode back out to the Layton ranch and checked the house first. Andy was there and said that Lonnie wasn't.

"Where did he go?"

"Who knows?" Andy asked. "Maybe he's out with those horses of his, only nobody can find them."

Fargo could. He remembered how to get there from when Andrea had taken him.

"Okay, thanks."

"What do you want with Lonnie?"

"Same thing I wanted with you, yesterday," Fargo said. "Just to ask some questions."

"Lonnie doesn't know anything," Andy said. "All he's interested in is women and horses."

"I'd like to see what he has to say, anyway."

"Suit yourself," Andy said, leaning on the door. "I've never known Lonnie to have anything to say that was worth listening to. He's really not very smart."

"I'll keep that in mind while I'm talking to him," Fargo said.

Andy closed the door and Fargo went back down the steps and mounted his borrowed gelding.

Since a sense of direction was extremely important to Fargo he was able to retrace the route Andrea had taken to Lonnie Layton's "secret" canyon. He rode through the fissure in the rock wall and into Lonnie's natural corral, and there he was. He was working with one of the horses, talking to it, apparently gentling it with the sound of his voice. Fargo paused to watch for a little while and gradually realized that Andy was wrong about his brother. Lonnie was apparently smart enough to have figured out a way to talk to horses so that they would listen. The longer Fargo watched Lonnie Layton patiently work with the horse, the more impressed he became.

Finally, Lonnie obviously felt he'd done enough with the animal because he walked away from it, but when he stopped short and just stood there with his back to the horse the colt came over and nudged him. Lonnie then turned and rubbed the colt's nose, and then his neck. Fargo was amazed that Lonnie had somehow gotten the horse to come to him, simply by turning his back.

Eventually Lonnie did walk away from the horse and he spotted Fargo watching.

"Well," he called out, "I guess they don't call you the Trailsman for nothing."

Fargo decided to let Lonnie believe he had found this place on his own. No point in starting trouble between brother and sister.

"I'm impressed," Fargo said, dismounting. "How did you do that?"

"Do what?"

"Get the horse to come to you?"

"I just had to convince him that he wanted to," Lonnie said. He opened the corral gate and came out, securing it behind him.

"What brings you here, Fargo?"

"I want to talk to you."

"About what?"

"Your brother, Tad."

"There's nothing to talk about," Lonnie said. "Tad's dead."

"Don't you want to know who killed him, and why?"

"It wouldn't do me any good to know who," Lonnie said. "You see, I'm not the vengeful type."

"What about the why?"

"Tad was not a pleasant man, Fargo," Lonnie said. "It's my bet that's why he was killed."

"What about your father?" Fargo asked. "He wants to know who and why."

"Only because somebody took something that belonged to him," Lonnie said. "He'd be just as upset if someone had stole a horse, or some cattle. See, nobody is supposed to get away with taking something that belongs to Big Ben Layton."

"What are we talking about here, Lonnie?" Fargo asked. "Your brother, some stock . . . or Karen Judd?"

Lonnie shrugged.

"Maybe all three."

"Talk to me a minute, Lonnie," Fargo said. "When did you see your brother last, that night?"

"When we rode into town," Lonnie said. "Then we all went our own way and I never saw him again. I didn't see anyone until Andrea found me the next morning."

"And you haven't heard of anyone having it in for Tad enough to kill him?"

"I told you before," Lonnie said. "Lots of people felt that way about Tad."

"Like Henry Judd?"

"Henry?" Lonnie laughed. "He wouldn't have the nerve. Besides, he could never take Tad."

"Not even if Tad was drunk?"

"I'd be real surprised if he did," Lonnie said.

"As a matter of fact," Fargo said, knowing he was taking a chance of maybe throwing Judd to the wolves here, "Henry says he had an argument with Tad that night and knocked him down."

"That's what he says."

"Uh-huh. He says he left him lying there, alive."

"Well, if that's what Henry says," Lonnie replied, "I believe him."

"Why's that?"

"Because Henry Judd is basically an honest man."

"I'm surprised to hear you say that."

"Why? Because he was feuding with my father? Or with Tad? If Henry had problems with either of them it was for a good reason. They both liked to push him, to see how far they could do it."

"And you don't think that maybe they finally pushed too far? That Henry snapped and killed Tad, maybe not only to get back at Tad, but at your father, too?"

"No."

"Why not?"

"You couldn't push Henry Judd that far."

"How do you know him so well?"

"I've lived here all my life, Fargo," Lonnie said. "I know the people."

"If that's true, then you can probably answer my questions better than you have been, Lonnie."

"I don't think so," Lonnie said. "There are just too many people in this valley who would have wanted Tad dead—or who would have killed him to get at my father. If I started naming names, I probably wouldn't know when to stop."

Fargo decided he believed Lonnie. It was odd, but he seemed to respect Henry Judd's honesty, which was probably something he didn't see a lot of growing up with Ben Layton as a father.

"Lonnie, did you shoot me and steal my horse?"

"Do you see your horse in there, Fargo?"

"No."

"I wouldn't steal a man's horse from him," Lonnie said. "If I wanted your horse I'd try to buy him from you."

Fargo believed him.

"Okay," Fargo said, and mounted the borrowed gelding.

"What kind of horse is he?"

"An Ovaro," Fargo said, "with distinctive markings," and he described them in detail, right down to the color of the saddle on the horse's back.

"I haven't seen an animal like that around here," Lonnie said. "I'd remember."

"Yes, I'm sure you would."

"I hope you find him," Lonnie said. "Stealing a man's horse, that's about as low as you can get."

Lower, apparently—in Lonnie's opinion—than killing somebody's brother.

14

By the time Fargo got back to town there was only one person he thought might be behind everything—his shooting, stealing his horse, and killing Tad. But it still couldn't have been done alone, so before he accused, he had to find the accomplice, as well.

Now he needed to make a list, for his own benefit, of possible accomplices.

He took the gelding to the livery, then walked back to the sheriff's office to see if Brannon was still there. He found the door locked, and there was no reply to his knock. He figured Brannon must be making his rounds, as it was dinnertime. He had two choices. Walk all over town and try to find him, or go and have dinner.

He opted for food. After he ate he could go to the saloon. Brannon was bound to show up there sooner or later. It would be part of his rounds.

He found a café he hadn't been to, went inside, and ordered a steak. He figured that was something you couldn't ruin. Well done or rare, a steak was edible.

He was wrong.

He went to the saloon after sawing through the steak for a while and then giving up on it. He ate the vegetables that came with it, had some coffee, and left with his teeth intact.

At the saloon—the same one he'd first seen Lonnie Layton in—he ordered a beer and drank it at the bar. The place was only half full, but that would change after dinner. That was when the husbands would flee their wives and take refuge either in the saloon, or in the arms of a whore in the local cathouse.

He was on his second beer when Sheriff Brannon came in and spotted him.

"Buy you one?" Fargo asked as the sheriff approached the bar.

"Why not?" Brannon asked. "It's still early for me to find trouble on my rounds."

Fargo signaled the bartender to bring another beer.

"Did you find Lonnie Layton?" Brannon asked, accepting the beer.

"I found him."

"And did he talk to you?"

"He did."

Brannon sipped his beer.

"And?"

"He had nothing to tell me."

"And what about your horse?"

"I don't think he had anything to do with that, either."

"What convinced you of that?"

"He did," Fargo said. "I watched him with a horse for a while. He's good, and he's got too much regard for them to steal another man's."

"Well," Brannon said, "sounds like Lonnie pretty much convinced you he's a little innocent."

"He convinced me he's a *lot* innocent."

"I mean—"

"I know what you meant," Fargo said. "Are you saying he's not innocent?"

Brannon shrugged. "Brothers have killed brothers before."

"Spare me the Cain and Abel story."

"There've been others."

"Then if it was one of his brothers who killed Tad," Fargo asked, "why not Andy?"

"Why not the old man?"

"What would his motive be?"

"He wants to be governor."

"He's pretty much going to be, isn't he?"

"Tad could have done a lot of damage to the Layton name."

Fargo frowned.

"Why would you want to pin this on Ben Layton?"

"My benefactor, you mean? Why not? I was thinking about it today. Once he leaves here to become governor who do you think will be in charge around here?"

"Andy?"

"That's right," Brannon said, "and Andy and me don't get along. How long do you think I'll be sheriff once the old man leaves?"

"So you'd rather see Ben leave for prison for killing his own son than for the governor's mansion?"

Suddenly, Brannon seemed to notice for the first time that they were in a public place. He put down his half finished beer and looked at Fargo.

"Forget it," he said. "I was just talkin'."

"Brannon," Fargo said, "how well do you know the Judds?"

128

"Well enough."

"Karen as well as Henry?"

"Well, no, I know Henry better—a lot better, actually. Why?"

"So you didn't know Karen before she married Henry?"

"I saw her with Ben," Brannon said, "but I didn't know her, no."

"I understand Karen pretty much went through the Layton men. Is that true?"

Brannon frowned.

"What are you drivin' at?"

"I'm just talkin'," Fargo said, "you know, like you."

"Well . . . I never heard of Karen havin' anything to do with Tad Layton. Everyone pretty much knows she was with Andy."

"What about Lonnie?"

"Lonnie's a ladies' man," Brannon said. "At least, he thinks so. It wouldn't surprise me if he chased after her."

"His father's wife-to-be?"

"Lonnie pretty much thinks with his dick half the time."

"And then she went on to Judd?"

"That's right."

"No stops in between?"

"Not that I—hey, you don't think I—hell, what would a woman like Karen Judd want with me?"

"Like I said," Fargo replied, "I'm just talking."

"Yeah, well, I ain't talkin' anymore," Brannon said. "Thanks for the beer. I got to finish my rounds."

"Sure, go ahead."

Brannon left and Fargo nursed the remainder of his beer, then ordered another.

"Heard you talkin' to the sheriff," the bartender said.

"Yeah?"

" 'Bout Karen Judd?"

"So what?"

"Could be I know somethin' useful."

"Could be?" Fargo asked. "Or you do?"

The man rubbed his hand over his face and said, "Could be."

"And when would I find out for sure?" Fargo asked.

The bartender looked around to see if anyone was within earshot.

"Mister, to tell you the truth I could use a few dollars."

"So you want to sell me the information?"

"If it's any good," the man said, "it might be worth somethin' to ya."

"How much?"

"I'll leave that up ta you," the man said. "If you don't think it's worth nothin', then don't pay me. Izat fair?"

Actually, it was more than fair. Fargo didn't like being hit up for money for information he didn't know was good or not and he was going to give the bartender a hard time before the man made his offer.

"It's more than fair," Fargo said. "What do you know, Dave?"

"Well," Dave said, leaning his elbows on the bar, "I knew Karen Engels before she came here."

"Karen Engels?"

"Karen Judd, now," Dave said. "See, I knew her in

130

Tucson when she was working in one of the houses there."

"Karen was a whore?"

"One of the best," Dave said.

Fargo could believe it, after the things she had done to him while he was flat on his back.

"Does anyone else know this?" Fargo asked.

Dave shrugged.

"I don't know if anyone else recognized her."

"I wonder if Ben Layton knew?"

"I'd say no," Dave said.

"Why?"

" 'Cause when she saw me here in town one time she nearly panicked and ran. Then she came up to me and begged me not to tell anyone."

"And you haven't?"

"Not a soul."

"You probably could have sold this information to Ben Layton before. Why didn't you?"

"Why would I wanna ruin Karen's chance with him?" Dave said. "Then, when that relationship broke up on its own, what was the point?"

"So then the question now is, Dave," Fargo asked, "why are you tellin' me?"

" 'Cause there's more to this story," Dave the bartender said, "and maybe it's got somethin' to do with Tad Layton's death."

"Okay, then," Fargo said, "tell me more . . ."

15

Fargo listened to what Dave the bartender had to say, gave him some money, and then went looking for Andrea Layton. If anyone in that family was gong to give him a straight answer, it would be her.

She wasn't in town so once again he had to take a ride out to the Layton ranch. Andy was in the corral next to the barn when he got there so he didn't bother going up to the house.

"What brings you back here?" Andy asked. "Couldn't find Lonnie?"

"I found him." Fargo dismounted and walked over to the corral.

"Then why are you back?"

"I'm looking for Andrea."

Now Andy approached the corral and leaned on the fence, on the opposite side of it from Fargo, but next to him so that they were almost facing one another.

"Is there something going on between you and my sister I should know about?"

Fargo wasn't sure how to answer that.

"If there was something going on between your sister and me," he asked, "why should you know about it?"

"Because she's my sister."

"Then maybe you should ask her that question," Fargo suggested. "Right now I'm looking for her to ask her a few of my own. Is she around?"

"I think I saw her ride out."

"So if I go up to the house I won't find her there?" Fargo asked, wondering if Andy was lying.

Andy looked at him and said, "Not if she went riding."

"What about Lonnie?" Fargo asked. "Have you seen Lonnie?"

"I thought you said you talked to him already."

"I did," Fargo said, "but maybe he saw Andrea."

"Well, I haven't seen Lonnie," Andy said. "If he was here it would mean he was working, and he's not here, is he?"

"I saw your brother work with his horses, Andy. He's very good."

"Really? I haven't seen it. Lonnie's just lazy, Fargo. All he cares about are those damn horses, and women."

"What did he think of Karen?"

The question surprised Andy.

"What?"

"Your brother Lonnie," Fargo said. "What did he think of Karen?"

"I don't understand—"

"As a woman, not as a potential stepmother."

"What are you trying to say?"

"Everyone says what a ladies' man your brother is," Fargo said. "I'm trying to find out what he thought of Karen Judd—or Engels—as a woman. Did he think she was pretty?"

"I don't—"

133

"Did he ever try to kiss her?"

"Wha—"

"Or do something else with her?"

"With Karen?"

"Why are you so puzzled by these questions?" Fargo asked. "Don't you think Karen is a beautiful woman? You must, you slept with her."

"That was diff—"

"Do you think she ever slept with your brother Lonnie?"

"No! Why would she?"

"Why would she sleep with you?"

"Because I loved her!" Andy shouted.

"You loved her?" Fargo asked after a moment. "But she was going to marry your father."

"I know that," Andy said. "Don't you think I know that? But I loved her from the first moment I saw her. She was so beautiful, and he's so . . . old."

"So you decided to steal her? To sleep with her?"

"No," Andy said, looking away. He turned his back and leaned against the corral. "It was her idea, not mine."

"But you didn't resist."

"No."

"And what happened after that?"

Andy laughed.

"Nothing," he said, "nothing happened. It was as if nothing had ever happened."

"But she broke her engagement to your father."

"Yes, but that had nothing to do with me. I thought it did, but it didn't."

"Maybe it had something to do with Lonnie? Or Tad?"

Andy looked at him now.

"You're thinking she slept with all of us? All the sons of the man she was going to marry?"

"I don't know," Fargo said. "Would she have done that, do you think?"

Andy thought about it a moment, looking miserable.

"I guess she could have," he said, finally. "Hell, why not? If she slept with me why not with them?"

"Why not?" Fargo asked. To find out the answer he'd have to ask Lonnie, or Karen. Or maybe Andrea knew.

"Why are you so interested in Karen?" Andy asked suddenly. "Do you think—you don't think she had anything to do with Tad's death."

"What do you know about her past, Andy?"

"Not much," he said. "Nothing, in fact. We never talked about it."

"And your father? What did he know about her?"

"Nothing, I guess. Why? What do you know about her?"

"Me?" Fargo asked. "Oh, nothing, I was just making conversation. I'm going to go and find your sister now."

Fargo mounted the gelding, turned it, and rode away from the ranch. He was convinced that Andy had not had any contact with Karen since she married Henry Judd, otherwise he wouldn't be so miserable talking about her. He was also convinced that the man still loved her. Karen might have been able to use him, if she wanted to, but Fargo decided that she hadn't.

If she did have something to do with Tad's death, then who had she used?

* * *

Fargo wondered what Karen would do to keep her past from coming out. She had apparently trusted Dave not to say anything. What if Tad had found out and was threatening to tell everyone? Still, what did that matter, unless Karen intended to try to hold on to her marriage?

Maybe the logical person to talk to now was Karen. Confront her, see what she said, and then move on. See if she could convince him that she had nothing at all to do with it, then he could go back to trying to find someone who had a grudge against Tad.

He turned the horse and headed for the Judd place.

When he arrived he looked around for a sign of Henry. Karen wouldn't admit anything if her husband was around. He went to the barn and looked inside. Henry's horse was gone. He rode to the house then, dismounted, and knocked on the door.

Karen answered the door.

"What do you want?" she demanded.

"I want to talk to you."

"About what?"

"Let me come inside."

"Henry's here—"

"No, he's not," Fargo said. "His horse is not in the barn. Let me in."

She backed away and allowed him to enter.

"If you intend to force yourself on me, forget it."

"I don't."

"What?" She seemed confused—or disappointed.

"I'm not here for that."

"Then why are you here?"

"To talk about you, and your past."

"My . . . past?"

"That's right."

"W-what do you know about my past?"

"Everything."

"I don't underst—"

"Tucson, Karen," he said, "I know about Tucson."

Her eyes narrowed, her face flushed, and she said, "Dave!"

"That's right."

"He promised me—I should have . . ."

"What? Killed him? Like you did Tad?"

She jerked back as if he'd slapped her.

"W-what are you talking about—Tad?"

"Did he find out about your past? Did he threaten to tell everyone? That would finish you in this town as a respectable woman, wouldn't it, Karen?"

She stared at him for a few moments, and then she started to laugh. It went on for some time, real belly laughs that brought tears to her eyes, and he watched her, trying to hide his confusion. Women, he thought.

"What's so funny?"

"You . . . are . . ." she said, gasping for air. "Do you . . . really think . . . I—I'm considered . . . re—respectable in this valley?"

And she started laughing again. He waited patiently, this time, for her to stop.

"Oh, my," she said, finally getting herself under control, "I haven't laughed like that in a long time."

"Seems to me it's at your own expense."

137

"Fargo, after what happened with Ben and Andy Layton no one in this town thinks I'm respectable— hell, even Henry didn't think so, and he married me."

"Tell me something, Karen," Fargo said, "since we're being so honest. Did you sleep with Tad and Lonnie, too, or just Andy? Just one son."

"Tad and Lonnie?" She looked at him like he was crazy. "Why would I sleep with them? Andy is the one who would inherit."

"That's why you slept with him?"

"Of course. He's the oldest son."

"But you were to be married to the father. When he died you'd get everything, wouldn't you?"

"Oh, no," she said, "Ben made it very clear that he would still leave the ranch to Andy."

"So you decided to concentrate on Andy."

"Only Ben found out," she said, "and he put a stop to it."

"But Andy loved you—he still does?"

"Did he tell you that?"

"He did."

"Hmmm," she said, thoughtfully, then. "No, it wouldn't have worked."

"Why not?"

"Because marrying Andy," she said, "would have been like marrying Andrea, as well."

"You mean because they're identical twins, and are close?"

"They're more than close, Fargo," she said. "They're much closer than brother and sister."

"What are you saying?"

"I think you know what I'm saying."

"You mean—"

"I mean," Karen said, "I wasn't about to share my marital bed with Andy *and* Andrea."

16

The information about Andy and Andrea was shocking, of course, but it didn't mean they were guilty of anything other than incest—if Karen was telling the truth. Of course, she could have been lying, but why? What did she have to gain?

"So you don't care if Henry finds out about your past?" Fargo asked.

"Of course I care," she said, "or I did, when I thought my marriage meant something and was going to last. Now, it doesn't really matter. We're just marking time."

"And the rest of the town? What if they found out?"

"I could care less what the people of this town think of me."

"And Ben Layton?"

She gave a short laugh now, not a belly laugh like earlier.

"Poor Ben. It would really shock him—although probably not as much as if he found out about his darling twins."

"How do you know about Andy and Andrea?"

"That's easy," Karen said. "Andy told me."

"He just came right out and told you?"

"Sure, why not? The poor jerk didn't think he'd

done anything wrong. See, nobody had ever told him that you're not supposed to have sex with your sister. He thought it was natural."

"And what did Andrea think?"

"Her? It was her idea. Andy said she crawled into bed with him when they were thirteen. She'd already had sex with some of the boys her age, and older, and she decided to try her brother—and apparently she liked it, because from then on they were exclusive."

"Exclusive? You mean—"

"I mean I was the first woman Andy'd had sex with other than his sister."

"Well, that would certainly give her reason to resent you, wouldn't it? Jealousy?"

"Oh, she resented me right from the start. I was threatening to come between her and her darling father. After all, they had a close relationship, as well."

"You don't mean—"

"No, I don't mean that," Karen said, "although who knows? Maybe Andrea was a very persuasive thirteen-year-old? Her mother was dead by then and she was the woman of the house. What do you think?"

"I don't know."

"Would that disgust you? To know that she was sleeping with her brother, and her father?"

"I think it would make me feel sorry for her," Fargo said, "and her family."

"Yeah," Karen said, "they're a pretty weird family, all right. That was the main reason I got out."

"Andy said his father called off the wedding because he found out about you two."

"That was convenient for him," she said. "I walked

141

away, so he passes the word that he canceled the wedding because he found out I was a slut. Imagine his surprise if he ever found out I was once a prostitute?"

"Well, he's not going to find out from me."

"That's very gentlemanly of you, Fargo," she said, "but is that why you really came here?"

"Why?"

"Because you found out about my past, and because you now have two good legs. I wondered all that time what it would be like with you when you were healthy, when you could be on top of me. Maybe we should find out now, huh?"

She came closer to him.

"Karen—"

She was undoing her dress.

"Karen—"

He could smell her skin, remember the feel and taste of it, of her. Now she was peeling the dress down from her shoulders, and her full breasts bobbed free, round and firm, the nipples hard.

"Karen, Henry could—"

"Henry will be gone all day, Fargo," she said huskily. "Come on, one last time, now that you're well and healthy. Come on, come on . . ."

The dress dropped to the floor and she was naked. The sharp odor of her readiness tickled his nose and he wanted her, he wanted her bad. . . .

She came into his arms and he lifted her easily, carried her into the room he'd stayed in. He was taking another man's wife—again—but he'd be damned if he'd take her in their bed, so he took her to the bed they'd shared before, when his movements were limited. Now there was no limit to what they could do.

He deposited her on the bed and started to take off his clothes.

"Hurry, hurry . . ." she was saying, pushing one hand down between her legs. "I'm ready for you, I'm ready . . . ready . . ."

And she was. He straddled her, the spongy head of his big cock pressed against her moist portal and then he was in her, sliding into her wetness so easily. His knees were on either side of her and she brought her legs up around his waist. He hadn't been able to move much the other times they'd had sex, so he intended to make up for it now. He began to slam into her, harder and harder, showing her what it was like when he had two good legs beneath him.

"Oooh, yes, uhn . . . uhn . . ." she grunted each time he banged into her, but it wasn't only taking her hard that was exciting. He slid his hands beneath her, cupped her buttocks and handled her as if she were a small woman, not the big woman that she was. His strength was such that she *felt* smaller, almost helpless in his arms, and she reveled in the fact that she was being *taken*, and that she was not in charge, that here was a man strong enough and forceful enough to handle her.

"Oh, yes, Fargo, yes, just take me, come on, harder . . . harder . . . mmm, mmm, mmm . . . oh, oh, oh . . ." She made all kinds of sounds, urging him on, and at one point actually sounded as if she were saying, "Yumm, yumm, yumm . . ."

He began to grunt then, with the force that he was using, and as the urge in him grew and he fought it down he grunted harder and harder, louder and louder, fighting the urge to explode and then totally unable to control it he went off like a geyser inside of her and she yelled as he filled her up, almost howling, clutching at him, scratching him, clutching him tighter still, milking him with her insides until he had nothing left to give her. . . .

"I'll bet it wasn't like that with little Andrea," she said later as she pulled her dress back on.

He had dressed in the bedroom, and then they walked into the kitchen, she naked, he walking behind her and getting the urge to take her again just by watching her hips sway, her butt twitch, and then she was pulling her dress back on.

"What makes you think I've been with Andrea?"

She laughed throatily, almost a chuckle, and said, "You have scratches I didn't give you."

Inadvertently he cast his eyes behind him, as if he could see.

"You know which scratches are yours?"

"A woman always knows, Fargo." She straightened her dress and faced him. "I don't think you should come back here, Fargo. For one thing, I might not be here, and for another, I don't think I'd be able to control myself. I'd be all over you again. If I had men like you coming to see me I'd have stayed a prostitute."

"I'll take that as a compliment."

"It was meant that way. Are you satisfied I didn't kill anyone?"

"Yes," he said.

"Why?"

"I'm not sure. Maybe because you didn't have a motive. Tad wasn't a threat to you. In fact, I can't see that anyone is, or was."

"I'm going to get out of this marriage and get out of this valley, Fargo. I don't think I want to stay in a place that would appoint Ben Layton governor, anyway."

"You don't think he'll make a good governor?"

"He'll make a great governor," she said. "He's a good politician, but that's *not* a compliment."

"I know what you mean."

She walked him to the door and outside.

"Karen, what about Henry? He admits to knocking Tad down while Tad was drunk, but says he didn't kill him."

"I believe him," Karen said. "You've got to look somewhere else, Fargo, and if I was you . . ."

"Yes?"

"I'd look inside the Layton family—deep inside."

"I've been thinking the same thing, Karen. Goodbye, and good luck."

"Hey," she said as he stepped down and started for his horse.

"Yeah?"

"I said don't come back here," she said, "but if we run into each other somewhere else, plan on giving me a whole day . . . and night."

"You got a deal."

"Oh, and there's one more thing you should know about your little friend, Andrea.

"And what's that?"

"She's a crack shot with a rifle," Karen said, "better than any of her brothers."

"That's interesting."

"I thought it might be."

Fargo mounted up and rode away from the Judd ranch, feeling that he would probably never return there. The Judds were clear, he thought, and he was going to take Karen's advice. He was going to look deep into the Layton family.

The only place to investigate the Layton family was the Layton ranch. As Fargo knew he'd gone to the Judd place for the last time, he planned for this to be his last trip to the Layton ranch. If the answers weren't there, then they weren't to be had. Who shot him, who stole his horse, where the Ovaro was, and who killed Tad Layton, all of these things, he felt, were to be answered there.

He rode up to the house and dismounted, leaving his horse loose. It wouldn't go far. He mounted the steps and knocked on the door. He was surprised when Lonnie answered it. He was also surprised that Lonnie was wearing a gun in the house.

"You again," the young man said. "Are you following me?"

"No," Fargo said, "I'm following the trail of your brother's killer."

"And you think it leads here?"

"I know it does."

"Well, who did it, then?" Lonnie asked. "Me? Andy? Andrea? Or did my father kill his own son?"

"Your father's the only one I know didn't do it," Fargo said. "Let me in and maybe we'll find out who did."

Lonnie hesitated a moment, then backed off to allow Fargo to enter. He closed the door and turned to face the much bigger man.

"Tell me what else you know, Fargo?"

"Well, for one thing," Fargo said, "you're a lot

smarter than anyone gives you credit for, and I think you like it that way."

"I guess that's a compliment," Lonnie said, "telling me that I play dumb."

"Not dumb," Fargo said, "but maybe a bit lazy, and girl crazy—you know, the footloose younger brother who doesn't want to work."

"And what does that prove?"

"Well, for one thing, I don't think you had anything against Tad."

"He was my brother."

"If I've learned one other thing," Fargo said, "it's that your family is not a normal family, so you don't have normal feelings about each other."

"Where is this leading?"

"I want to question everyone," Fargo said. "Andrea, Andy, and your father. I want to get to the bottom of this today."

"Well," Lonnie said, "if you want to get to the bottom of it I guess you better talk to Father. He usually has all the answers. Follow me."

17

Lonnie Layton showed Fargo the way to his father's office. They went down a hall toward the back of the house and then entered a room. Ben Layton was seated behind a desk in a room dominated by books. They lined all four walls, more books than Fargo had ever seen in one place.

"Mr. Layton," he said, "I have some questions to ask you and the members of your family . . ."

Fargo stopped when he realized that the older man wasn't listening. In fact, from the look in the man's eyes, he wasn't even aware that Fargo was in the room.

"What's wrong with him?"

"He has his lucid moments," Lonnie said. "He goes in and out. You've only seen him during his good moments—up till now."

Fargo turned to face Lonnie. As he did so both Andy and Andrea entered the room. Both were wearing guns.

"But what's wrong with him?" he asked, again.

"We don't know," Andrea said. "He just . . . loses his mind, sometimes."

"How long has this been going on?"

"Just about a year," Andrea said, "maybe a little longer."

"Who knows about this?" Fargo asked.

"No one," Andy said. "We've managed to keep it from everyone."

"From Karen?"

"It wasn't happening when she was around," Andrea said. "She doesn't know."

"But . . . he's supposed to be governor."

"He will be governor," Andrea said.

"We won't let anyone stop that from happening," Andy said.

"Not even Tad," Lonnie said.

And suddenly everything was clear to Fargo.

"You all did it," he said. "You all killed your brother."

"Tad was a disgrace," Lonnie said.

"His behavior could have cost Father the governorship," Andrea said.

"We couldn't let that happen," Andy chimed in.

"But, why did he send for me?"

The three siblings exchanged looks.

"We don't know why," Andrea said. "He managed to do it without us knowing. We didn't realize it until you were on your way here."

"Then one of you shot me," Fargo said.

"I did," Andrea said. "I wasn't trying to kill you, just get you to go away. My bullet creased your skull by accident. It was a fluke. I usually hit what I'm aiming at."

"It's different when it's a man," Fargo said, "even if you're trying to miss."

"I'm sorry," she said. "We wanted you to go away."

"And what about my horse?" Fargo asked. "Keeping it wasn't the way to get me to go away."

"We didn't know that," Andy said.

"Lonnie liked the horse," Andrea said. "It was a mistake." As she said it she threw a look at her younger brother.

"Where is the horse?" Fargo asked.

"I have it hidden," Lonnie said. "Andrea purposely took you to one of my corrals to try to convince you that I didn't have it, but I have others."

"Why not let me have it back?" Fargo asked. "I might have gone away, then."

"We didn't think so," Andrea said. "I thought you'd keep looking for whoever shot you."

"And now I've found you," Fargo said. "Found who shot me—" Andrea. "—who took my horse—" Lonnie. "—and who killed Tad." All of them.

"And now we can't let you leave," Andy said.

"We're sorry, Fargo," Andrea said.

"Yeah," Lonnie said, and the three of them went for their guns.

Fargo was not a fast-draw artist, and even if he was he might not have been able to take the three of them in that small room. Instead of going for his own gun, then, he went for the window. He dove through it, shattering it. When he landed he jarred his back, but ignored it. He rolled to his feet and ran for cover as the three Layton siblings ran to the window and started firing at him.

He sought cover behind a horse trough by the corral. He was on the side of the house, away from where he'd left the gelding.

Andrea, Andy, and Lonnie all climbed out the window and fanned out, finding cover. They effectively had Fargo pinned down, and he had a problem.

Apparently, jumping through the window and landing hard had affected his lower back, and suddenly his legs were feeling numb. In a matter of moments he lost all feeling in them, and he couldn't have stood if he wanted to.

He was in a bad way, in more ways than one.

They kept him pinned down by firing at him every so often. The bullets harmlessly punched into the horse trough, creating holes through which the water started to leak out. Enough of those and his cover might become useless, if all the water managed to drain out.

He still hadn't drawn his own weapon or returned any fire, so he took his Colt out of his holster and dragged himself to one end of the horse trough. He peered around and tried to spot the triumvirate of Laytons.

He'd thought that all three had come out the window. He was wrong. Andrea was still inside, but she was peering out the window and firing her gun. If Karen was right about her, she was not as deadly with a pistol as she was with a rifle.

Andy had taken cover around the corner of the house, to the left of the window where Andrea was. Fargo had seen him shoot. He did pretty well with bottles and cans, but there was no telling how well he'd do against a man.

That left Lonnie, who had taken cover beneath a buckboard that had only three wheels. Obviously, it was awaiting repairs, but for now it was cover. Lonnie was lying beneath it, his gun in his hand.

Fargo could see all three of them, and if he'd had his legs beneath him he felt sure he could take them. This was not where they were at their best. They probably excelled in covering for their father, who was apparently senile, or ill. They had been so intent on covering for him, and making sure that he got his governorship, that they had even killed their own brother. Apparently, there was more family unity in the Layton family than he had previously thought, except that Tad was the odd sibling out.

Fargo was willing to bet that the brains of the whole family—now that Ben was apparently losing his—was Andrea.

"Andrea!" Fargo shouted. "Let's talk this out."

"There's nothing to talk about, Fargo," she called back. "There's no way we can let you go. You'll tell people about Tad, and about Father's illness. We can't allow that."

"Tad's already dead, Andrea," Fargo said. "Do you want to lose any more brothers?"

"There's three of us and one of you," Andrea said. "You can't get away."

"I'll take at least one of you with me," Fargo called back. "Who will it be? You? Andy? Lonnie?"

"Lonnie!" Andrea shouted. "You charge him, we'll cover you."

"Yeah, Lonnie," Fargo shouted, "you be the one to come out in the open, not one of the twins. They wouldn't risk each other, would they? Not as close as they are."

"Shut up, Fargo!" Andrea yelled. "Lonnie! Go on. We'll cover you."

"Come on, Lonnie," Fargo said, "let's see how well they cover you."

There was some hesitation on Lonnie's part as he thought things over.

"Andy," he finally shouted, "you charge him and we'll cover you."

"No!" Andrea snapped. "Not Andy. You, Lonnie."

"Why me?" Lonnie asked. "Because I'm expendable? Because I'm not a twin?"

"Lonnie," Andy chimed in, "we've got to get him. Come on, you and me can both charge him while Andrea lays down cover."

"No!" Andrea shouted again. "Not you, Andy!" She was obviously concerned for her twin—much more concerned than she was for her other brother. "Lonnie, damn it, you do what I tell you! We've got to get him before Dack Sessions and the hands get back!"

"Forget it, Andrea," Lonnie said, "I'm not taking all the risks."

"Lonnie, let's do it on three," Andy shouted. "Both of us."

"Both of us?" Lonnie called.

"That's what I said."

"Okay," Lonnie said, "you count."

"Andy, no!" Andrea wailed, but it was too late.

And Fargo knew what was going to happen.

"One . . . two . . . three!" Andy shouted, and he charged.

Lonnie, not sure he could trust his brother, held back, and Andy was left out in the open.

Andrea started to fire at the horse trough, but she didn't know which side Fargo was on. Fargo, on his belly because he couldn't stand or even kneel with his useless legs, fired several times. One shot took Andy in the knee and dragged him down. Another hit him square in the chest as he stumbled.

"Andy's hit!" Lonnie shouted.

"Noooo!" Andrea wailed, and came crawling out the window. She fell to the ground, then got to her feet and ran toward her twin.

"Andrea, watch out!" Lonnie yelled, but she was beyond hearing.

Fargo had no choice but to fire at her while she was in the open. In his condition he had to shoot to kill, and that was what he did. His first shot hit her in the chest, the second in the shoulder. It was the first one that stopped her dead in her tracks, though. She got a puzzled look on her face, frowned, and said, "Andy?" once, and then fell on her face in the dirt.

"That's two, Lonnie," Fargo said. "You're three."

"You son of a bitch!" Lonnie shouted. "Come on out, Fargo!"

"You come and get me, Lonnie."

Fargo had fired four shots. He hurriedly ejected the empties from his gun and reloaded all six chambers while Lonnie thought over his next move.

"Come on, Lonnie," Fargo called, "I don't have all day."

"Your horse back, Fargo?" Lonnie called out. "Your fancy horse?"

That stopped Fargo.

"Andrea shot you, but I've got your horse. I'll tell you where it is, but you got to let me go."

"Where are you going to go, Lonnie?"

"I don't know," Lonnie said, sounding panicky, "but I ain't gonna die for the old man. Andrea was the one who wanted him to be governor. I don't give a damn."

Fargo remained silent. He could tell from Lonnie's voice that the younger man was going to become impatient and do something foolish.

"What do you say, Fargo?"

"Where is the horse, Lonnie?"

"Uh-uh," Lonnie said. "You let me go first."

"And how will I find the horse?"

"I'll climb back in the window and leave a note on the desk. I'll leave a map so you can find it."

There was no guarantee that Lonnie would do that, at all. As badly as Fargo wanted his horse back, he couldn't let the man out of his sight.

"You tell me where the animal is, Lonnie," he shouted, "and we'll talk."

"Goddammit, Fargo!"

Fargo remained silent again. Lonnie had to make up his mind what he was going to do.

"Fargo, I'll go the window and get the old man to give me a pencil and some paper. I'll write the map and leave it right by the window. I'll weigh it down so it don't blow away. What do you say?"

Andrea was dead, and Fargo knew that she was the one who had shot him. All he'd wanted was the person who had shot him, and his horse, and he was damn close to getting both.

"Okay, Lonnie," Fargo said. His legs were tingling as the feeling started to return. "Go to the window and do it. If you try to climb into the house I'll kill you."

"You got my word, Fargo."

"Then do it."

Tentatively, Lonnie came from around the corner of

the house. He was tense, expecting Fargo to fire, and when he didn't he became emboldened. He walked to the window, his gun still in his hand.

"I'm just gonna lean in to talk to the old man," he called.

"Go ahead." Fargo could feel his legs now. He thought that in a few moments he'd be able to move them.

He watched as Lonnie moved to the window and leaned in. He couldn't hear what was being said, but Lonnie had apparently only gotten a few words out when there was a shot from inside the house. Lonnie was jerked backward as if someone had pushed him. He staggered a few feet, then fell onto his back, dead.

Fargo moved his legs, trying to get them beneath him. He used the horse trough to push himself to his feet, staggered once, then gathered them beneath him. He started to walk stiffly toward the house, wondering who had fired the shot from inside.

He stopped to look at Andy and Andrea, both of whom were dead, then walked to Lonnie. He was on his back with a hole in his forehead, also dead.

Fargo walked to the house. As he got there Ben Layton appeared in the window with a gun. Fargo tensed, ready to fire if the man made a threatening move.

"What's going on?" Layton yelled. "Who was that trying to climb in my window?"

Fargo continued to approach the window, slowly, warily, but there was no danger. The gun was dangling loosely from Ben Layton's hand and Fargo was able to grab it away from him.

"It's all over, Mr. Layton."

"Huh?" Layton frowned. "Is that you, Fargo? What's going on?"

"Your family tried to kill me, Layton," Fargo said. "Andy, Andrea, and Lonnie, they killed Tad."

"What? They killed their brother? Why?"

"To make sure you became governor."

"I am going to be governor," Layton said.

Fargo doubted it, but he kept quiet.

"Fargo? They're all dead?"

"All of them, Layton."

Ben Layton thought that over for a few moments, and then he said, "They were ungrateful whelps, anyway."

"If you say so," Fargo said. He leaned against the house, his legs still shaking, and holstered his gun. He tossed Ben Layton's gun away. "I just wish Lonnie would have told me where my horse was before he died."

"Your horse?"

"Yes."

"The Ovaro?"

"That's right."

"Hell," Layton said, "I know where your horse is."

He did, too, and he told Fargo.

1860, the New Mexico Territory,
where the southern end of the
Sangre de Christo Mountains edged the
vast plains and looked down on a new
and deadly kind of cattle drive . . . .

The big man's lake blue eyes were darkened as he scanned the jagged reaches of the Sangre de Christo mountain range. These brutal peaks harbored a thousand ways to kill, he knew. Every crag, rock pinnacle, pointed boulder, and sloping talus could bring sudden death. Every path, defile, twisting, torturous passage could plunge a horse and rider over one of the naked cliffs of sheer rock. Nature lay in wait for every intruder, ready to strike with a loose rock, an unexpected hole, a crumbling cliffside, death and danger multiplied in countless ways. And the cruel mountains were host to those who offered death in their own ways.

For the careless, sidewinders waited with their

venom-filled fangs, as did the tiger rattler, the Mojave
and blacktail rattler, and the coral snake, as attractive
as it was deadly. For the unwary, the mountain lion
could kill with one silent pounce and for the tired, the
red wolf pack was relentless in pursuing its prey. In
the hard, harsh mountains of the Sangre de Cristo
range, humans were simply one more potential victim
for the land and all its denizens of fang, claw, and
talon. And now one more way for death to strike had
appeared. Sky Fargo's mouth became a thin line as he
scanned the sky, took in the deep purple-gray of it, the
very color menacing. He ran one hand along the jet
black neck of the magnificent Ovaro as the horse's ears
twitched nervously, instinct signaling danger. "Easy,
old friend," he murmured as his gaze swept the vast
expanse of the lowering clouds.

The sky would open up soon, he knew, bursting
open with a fury of its own to send a deluge of water
down on every crag, peak, and path in the mountains.
A terrible, pounding deluge would follow and send
cascades of water racing down to fill every cranny, defile, crevice, path, and road that threaded through the
mountains. He had witnessed these fierce storms before, knew how it would grow in power as more and
more rain poured unceasingly down onto the land.
Torrents of water would consume everything in its
path, dislodging sloping taluses, sending rock hurtling
downward, sweeping away pieces of loose crag, and
flinging more rocks in all directions. Only shelter
could keep a man alive, the right shelter in the right
place. He had ridden these mountains before, not
often yet enough times and to him, a trail, a pathway,

a passage, was forever imprinted in his mind, that special mind of a trailsman where the land was a book, a map, words and sentences made of earth, leaf, and tree. He had drawn on those imprints of nature, visualized the shelter that would keep him alive during the storm. It was one of the few places offering survival and he turned the pinto down a narrow passage, came out at the end of it on a level stretch. He rode till he recognized another short cutoff, and took it to another passage that bordered high rocks on one side, mountain brush on the other. A tall spire of granite was a remembered beacon and he rounded the path beside it. The first hard spray of rain suddenly flung itself into his face and he kept the Ovaro at a slow trot, glanced at twisted paloverde trees that somehow grew out of the mountainsides in stunted, misshapen forms. He rode on as the sky continued to fling intermittent sprays of rain at him with a kind of malicious playfulness. He'd gone perhaps another hundred yards when he caught the sound, unmistakable, and he reined to a halt, peering down over the edge of the path. The wagon raced along the narrow roadway below, one side of the road a sheer cliff, and he watched it careen perilously close to the edge as it rounded a tight curve. He frowned at the rig, a closed-panel rockaway, drawn by two horses. It was no wagon for these mountains, not at any time, and now it was a rolling coffin going the wrong way in the wrong place.

He spurred the Ovaro forward, found a narrow, winding defile, and sent the horse down it until he emerged on the roadway below. He reined to a halt, peered over the edge of the sharp drop on one side, grimaced as he saw but a few hardy brush growths and the rest uneven sides of rock. The wagon came into sight moments later and he raised a hand. The wagon drew to a halt as he blocked its path and Fargo felt the furrow dig into his brow as he saw a smallish figure holding the reins, loose, dark brown hair flowing around a round-cheeked, soft face. The young woman sat motionless as he started to move closer and he saw a curtain behind her. He gestured with one hand at the sky. "You're going to get yourself killed damn soon," Fargo said. Suddenly the curtain came open and another figure pushed forward, dark brown hair worn tight and swept upward atop her head, a long, lean face and Fargo saw the big plains rifle in the young woman's hands.

"Hell we are, damn you," the woman said as she brought up the rifle.

"Shit," Fargo swore as the shot exploded and he flung himself sideways from the saddle. He felt the shot whistle past his shoulder as he hit the ground, rolled, and stopped just at the edge of the cliffside. The Ovaro backed up and Fargo glanced up to see the young woman bring the rifle around for another shot. A quick glance told him there was no place to hide and he rolled, letting himself go over the side as the second shot smashed into the rock. He fell, reached out, hit a protruding rock, managing to close his hand around a scrubby branch and halt his fall. He heard the wagon roll forward, the young woman's voice cutting through the thick, turgid air. "He was one of them. Let's get out of here," she said and Fargo heard the snap of the reins on the team, the scrape of wagon wheels on stone.

Cursing silently, he kept his grip on the length of scrub branch, using his other hand to find a crack in the rock. Slowly, he pulled himself upward, groping until he found another tiny ledge that afforded a fingerhold. He felt the branch bend as he pulled on it, paused, pulled again, and gave a sigh of relief as the branch held. Exerting a careful, steady pull, Fargo clung to the branch, lifted himself, found another tiny ledge of rock, and climbed again until he reached the edge of the roadway. He pulled one leg up, crawled over the top of the cliffside, and pushed to his feet. He found the Ovaro at once, a dozen yards away against the high rocks at one side of the road. The wagon had found the room to squeeze by and had gone on. Another spray of rain struck at Fargo as he walked to the horse.

But this time the spray was followed by a steady pelting of rain. The skies were beginning to open up, Fargo noted. Drawing his rain slicker from the saddlebag, he donned it and swinging onto the pinto, stared down the mountain road where the two young women had vanished. They'd plainly been afraid of something but the one had been too damn quick to shoot. She'd almost killed him and he'd no inclination to let her try again. He'd stopped to offer help and had damn near taken a bullet for it. The hell with them, he thought. Whatever their problems, whatever their fears, they'd have to live with them. And their own stupidity. In this case, die with them, he thought grimly. Death would most surely catch up to them.

There was no hiding place, no safe refuge down the road they had taken. The area was one of cliffs, sheer drops, and granite walls with shallow overhangs that would prove to be death traps when the cascading waters began to rise and fill the narrow pathways.

He turned the Ovaro down a side passage and refused to feel guilty. You couldn't be everyone's keeper, he told himself as he increased the pinto's pace. He let the feeling of his own survival pull at him. After all, he had to reach his own refuge and that could elude him if the storm grew too fierce too quickly, rain and wind obscuring details of marks and signposts that were at best unclear. The rain had begun to come down steadily and he could feel the wind picking up speed. He peered hard through the raindrops at passing rock formations as he made his way down another passage. Suddenly he found what he sought, a narrow path that split off from the wider passage to wind up alongside a high wall of rock. Halfway up, the rock grew less severe, becoming a series of overhangs and deep indentations, scrubby trees dotting the terrain. A few hundred yards on he saw the mouth of the cave, set back from the passage and tall enough for a horse and rider to enter.

It had given him shelter once before, that time from a pursuing band of Comanches, and he steered the Ovaro into the deep, tall cave, high enough and back far enough to escape the torrent of water that would engulf the land. He dismounted and explored the cave in the light still remaining. It was relatively clean, only a few carcass bones littering the sides. Outside of the dankness common to all caves, it didn't stink of raccoon or skunk urine or the pungent odor of bear. The black bears that wandered high into the mountains preferred smaller, tighter caves for hibernation. Stepping to the mouth of the cave, he peered out at the rain that came down at a slant now, driven by new winds. The storm had strengthened, the rain drumming a tattoo against the rocks. He let another minute go by as the mixed feelings continued to churn inside him.

His lips a tight line, he turned suddenly, strode to the pinto, and pulled himself into the saddle, cursing the two young women, who were victims about to happen, and himself. A conscience was a meddlesome, troublesome affliction. It made a man defy his better judgment, ignore common sense, and indulge in efforts he'd no need to take. Damn the thing, he swore as he sent the pinto out of the cave. The rain assaulted him at once and he wiped at his eyes as he peered up at the sky, estimating that he had a half hour, perhaps, before the water started down from the high peaks to race through every passageway. Keeping the horse at a slow trot, he went down the road and felt the rain increase in power. The road turned and twisted, one side high rock, the other a cliffside with a sheer drop to death far below on jagged boulders.

He kept the Ovaro against the high rock side as the road narrowed, his lips pulled back as precious minutes ticked away. He had carefully rounded a half-dozen curves when he went around the second of a pair of extremely sharp twists. As he came out of the curve he reined up sharply. The wagon rose up before him, on its side, the two horses still with it, held in place by their twisted harnesses. They pawed the ground and strained against the straps holding them, frightened, aware of death with that sixth sense all animals possess. Fargo dismounted, strode over to them, and calmed them both with his hands and voice as he peered at the overturned wagon. The rockaway lay at the very edge of the cliffside, the front almost hanging over the edge. It had plainly skidded as it took the curve too fast and went over, the front panels broken and knocked out. He stepped to the rig and peered inside. Neither of the two young women was there and he drew back, wondering if they'd fled on foot in panic. He peered at the broken panels again.

They had been knocked outward. Bodies had been flung through them when the wagon overturned. He stepped around the back of the rockaway to the edge of the cliff, squinted downward, taking a moment to adjust his vision to the rain. The narrow ledge of rock took shape some fifteen feet below him, then the two figures clinging to it. They had miraculously landed on the only ledge that jutted out of the otherwise sheer wall of rock. A few feet to the right or left and they'd have plunged to their deaths at the bottom of the drop. They lay flat on the ledge, he saw, clinging precariously, and he saw one wave up at him with one arm. Cupping his hands to his mouth, he called through the noise of the wind and the rain. "Can you get up?" he asked.

The answer came back as from very far away. "It's wet and slippery." His lips drew back in a grimace. The ledge would grow wetter and more slippery the harder the rains came. When the floodwaters raced down the road they'd spill over the side and sweep the two figures from the ledge. Fargo turned, hurried to the Ovaro, and took the rope from the lariat strap. He began to wrap it around his hand as he returned to the edge of the cliff, then fashioned a noose at the other end. Dropping to one knee, he began to lower the lariat. When it reached the ledge, the smaller figure reached one arm up, grasped the rope, and pulled it to her. "Put the loop around your waist," Fargo called down. He waited as she brought the noose down to her waist. When it was in place, he pulled it tight around her. "Now hold on to the rope with both hands," he said, bracing himself against the rear of the overturned wagon.

She obeyed, bringing both hands to the rope, and he felt her slip from the ledge at once. But he was prepared, his powerful shoulder muscles tightened as the full weight of her pulled on his arms, shoulders, and back. He let her swing against the side of the cliff, hang there for a moment, and then began to pull her up. He pulled slowly, steadily, straining his back and arms. His lips drew back as he felt the rain causing his grip on the rope to slip. He heard the girl's short scream of panic as she dropped in space while he wound another turn of the rope around his hands. Starting to pull again, he felt her scraping along the face of the rock wall as he pulled her upward. She was unable to do anything but cling to the rope and hang helplessly, he realized, and he pulled harder with muscles that protested. The rain had grown stronger, hitting against him in a steady, wind-driven assault.

But finally, he saw the top of her head appear over the edge of the cliffside, then the rest of her slowly come into sight. When her shoulders reached the edge of stone, she reached out, found a finger grip, and began to pull herself onto the road. He loosened the pull on the lariat, skidded himself almost on his back, and closed one hand around her arm and helped pull her onto the road. She lay prone for a moment, drawing in deep breaths of air as he pushed onto one knee and loosened the rope from around her waist, finally pulling it free of her. Her loose, brown hair was rain-soaked but it somehow remained full around her round face. She was a smallish, compact figure, he noted briefly. "Stay right here," he told her as he went back to the end of the cliff and began to lower the lariat again.

The other young woman lay flat on the ledge, plainly not daring to move, and he maneuvered the lariat until it dropped onto her. "Take it, put it around your waist," he called. The young woman reached one hand out, brought the noose down, began to pull it around her waist. She reached up with her other hand and as she did, her feet slipped on the wet rock. He yanked hard to close the noose as she went over the edge with a scream, the feel of her sudden weight pulling against his arms. "Damn," he spit out as he slid forward on the wet stone, his body only inches from the edge. Keeping his grip on the rope, he rolled, and holding his arms over his head, found a few inches more as the road curved and managed to get one heel up against a small rise of stone. It was enough to keep him from being pulled over the edge as he pushed hard against it, sweat mingling with the rain coursing down his face.

He rested a moment, took in a deep breath, and felt the figure swinging in the air at the other end of the rope. He felt for the young woman's panic, unable to do anything but hang helplessly in midair. Slowly, he gathered his strength again and began to pull. He cursed at the rain that continued to make his grip on the rope slip. Casting a quick glance at the young woman who sat against the wagon, he saw that she was frozen in place, staring with her eyes wide. "Get over here," Fargo shouted. His sharp cry snapped the half trance and she blinked, swung herself around, and crawled to him. "Take a hold and pull, dammit," he rasped and she grasped the lariat a few inches in front of his hands. "Every little bit helps," he muttered as his muscles cried out again as he took a long pull. Looking at the rope where it scraped against the edge of the cliffside, he was grateful to see it had not frayed yet.

Though time passed as usual, it seemed made of lead as the girl pulled with him and he was glad for what little she contributed. His arms seemed ready to pull out of their shoulder sockets when the young woman's head appeared, then her shoulders. "Give her a hand," Fargo ordered. Finding a reservoir of strength in his straining muscles, he leaned back in order to keep the rope taut. The girl crawled to the edge of the cliff, lying flat as she reached out with both arms and closed hands around her friend's shoulders. She pulled as the other young woman drew one leg up and half pushed herself onto the top of the road and safety. Fargo let the lariat go limp and heaved a deep breath of his own. He moved to the young woman, who lay prone beside the wagon, loosened the noose, and lifted it from her as she looked up at him, gratitude flooding her face.

A long, thin face, not at all like the other girl's, Fargo noted as he extended a hand, helping her to her feet. She was a lot taller than the other girl, her figure lean, her hair swept up atop her head, as he had seen when he glimpsed her in the wagon. The heavy rain made a good look at her impossible and he straightened, his voice hard. "Let's go. We're on borrowed time," he said. "Unhitch the horses. You'll be riding them."

"Get our bags," the taller girl said to the other as she strode to the horses and began to undo the harness and reins. Fargo went to the Ovaro and swung onto the saddle as the round-faced girl came from the wagon carrying to leather traveling bags.

"You ever ride bareback?" Fargo asked them both.

"Yes," the tall one said and the other nodded agreement.

"This time you'll be riding wet on a wet horse. We'll stay at a walk," Fargo said. "We've no time to have you sliding off every few minutes." He watched both young women pull themselves onto the horses, each with a bag slung over one shoulder. They managed to mount without problems, and came alongside him as he sent the Ovaro back down the road. At least two inches of water now coursed atop the road, he saw, and cursed silently. The two inches would soon be six feet of racing water, pushed by thousands of pounds of force from the high peaks, made even more powerful as it channeled through narrow passages. Fargo shot a rainswept glance at the sky. Daylight still clung but it was a dark, threatening, glowering daylight and Fargo forced himself to keep the pinto at a walk. The rain bounced from his rain slicker and as he shot a glance at the two young women, he saw the round-faced one shiver as she rode. Fargo made his way back the way he had come and when he reached the road that turned off upward to the cave, the water flowed ankle-deep against the pinto's legs.

Fargo led the way up the narrow incline to the cave, and rode into the high-ceilinged shelter. He swung from the saddle as the two young women followed him in. He pulled his rain slicker off as the two women slid from their horses and he had a chance to properly look at them for the first time. The smaller, round-faced one had a soft prettiness to her, even soaked as she was. Her blouse clung to high breasts that somehow echoed the roundness of her face, two little points pushing sharply into the wet fabric. Dark brown eyes gazed back at him from a pretty, almost babyish face, full lips adding to the picture.

His glance went to the other young woman. She had none of the round-faced prettiness of the first one, her face long and angular with a straight nose and almost prim mouth. Yet there was a strong attractiveness in it, high cheekbones giving her a chiseled imperiousness. Her soaked blouse also rested against her breasts, but these were long, slow-curving mounds that fitted the rest of her lean, narrow body, torso, hips, legs, all of flowing symmetry. Only the cool severity of her marred what might be a patrician kind of beauty, he decided. The round-cheeked one spoke up first.

"We're soaked to the skin and cold. We've dry clothes in our bags. We want to change," she said.

"Go ahead," he grunted.

"We're not inclined to put on a show," the tall one said.

"Go back deep into the cave. It'll be too dark there for me to see you," he said.

They nodded in unison and he watched them go to their traveling bags and take out towels and dry clothes. They walked together back into the interior of the cave, where they faded away in the darkness where no daylight penetrated. He went to the mouth of the cave and stared out at the water rushing past on the road below, already nearing four feet in height. He watched it churn, spit foam, and bubble and he turned only when he heard the sound behind him. Both young women stood before him in dry clothes, peering at him, the round-faced one with open curiosity, the tall, lean one with severity. She spoke first, this time. "Why'd you come back?" she asked.

"Because I'm not whoever the hell you thought I was, honey," he tossed back. "And I've a conscience that makes me protect damn fools." He turned, strode to the edge of the cave entrance, and motioned to them. They came and halted beside him, their eyes widening as they stared down at the rushing torrent of water that had risen another foot higher. "That's where you'd be, swept away in that, and it's going to get worse," he said. "If you hadn't skidded and overturned you'd be swept away and drowning by now."

The smaller one swallowed hard and stepped back as a gust of wind pelted her with rain. Her eyes fastened on him. "Thank God for your conscience," she murmured. He stepped back and she went with him as the taller one followed. "I'm Angela Carter. This is my sister, Amanda. You can be surprised. Everybody is. We don't look like sisters."

"I'm not surprised," Fargo said and she raised an eyebrow. "I've seen that before with sisters," he finished. "I'm Fargo . . . Skye Fargo. Some people call me the Trailsman. Now, you want to tell me what you were doing in a rockaway up in these mountains?"

"Trying to take a shortcut down to the plains east of here instead of going the long way around," Angela said.

"Damn fools. I'll say it again," Fargo snapped. "That's no rig for these mountains. No wonder it went over at the first chance."

"We thought it'd be faster than a heavy mountain wagon," Angela said.

Fargo's lake blue eyes wore a coating of frost as he turned them on Amanda. "That doesn't explain why you took two shots at me," he growled.

"I thought you were trying to stop us," Amanda said.

"From going through the mountains?" He frowned.

"From reaching our herd on the plains," she answered.

Fargo's frown stayed as he sat down on the floor of the cave. Angela quickly followed suit, folding her compact figure down across from him, her soft, round face warm and open. Amanda stayed standing, cool, contained appraisal in her face, and Fargo found himself wondering how two pairs of brown eyes could be so different. "I think you'd better start at the beginning," he said.